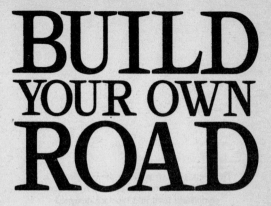

BUILD
YOUR OWN
ROAD

How to Define
Your Goals...
and Design a Path
to Reach Them

Lois Wolfe-Morgan

BERKLEY BOOKS, NEW YORK

BUILD YOUR OWN ROAD

A Berkley Book / published by arrangement with
Creative Services, Inc.

PRINTING HISTORY
Executive Press edition published 1990
Berkley edition / February 1992

ISBN: 0-425-13186-6

A BERKLEY BOOK® TM 757,375
Berkley Books are published by The Berkley Publishing Group,
200 Madison Avenue, New York, New York 10016.
The name "BERKLEY" and the "B" logo
are trademarks belonging to Berkley Publishing Corporation.

PRINTED IN THE UNITED STATES OF AMERICA

10 9 8 7 6 5 4 3 2 1

IN MEMORY OF Dennis Michael Lyden—
my brother, my friend, and a courageous
man who gave his life in Vietnam in March 1966.

With a special love to my parents—
Muriel and Lawrence Lyden.

And

Dedicated to Michael Henry Morgan III,
my husband.

Foreword

"Those not interested need not apply." The subtlety of the want-ad line generally escapes our thoughts relative to employment, but Lois Wolfe-Morgan's *Build Your Own Road* does not have to be interpreted. While this line shouts the obvious, we generally have to stop and think through it to get the message which is very similar to road-building commitments.

Lois and I had a unique opportunity to share some of our professional career together. Her creativity, intuition, and professionalism is so refreshing as you will quickly identify in this book. As we shared our careers we also shared our personal road building in a very supportive and developing way. We really became mentors for one another and we have continued that support in spite of our professional lives leading in different directions. We frequently reminded each other of road building strategies with the following quips: Happiness (Anger, fear, etc.) is a choice; Happiness is not a station in life, but a manner of travel; Don't wait for it to happen, make it happen.

Building your own road is a matter of choice but is different than other life development experiences, i.e.

formal education or basic training in the military. Once you have completed basic training or your formal education you don't return for repeat performances, when it's done, it's done. But everyday living sends you back for basic training every once in a while. Unless you have control of building your own road, life's events can confuse us with what road we are traveling—maybe it is someone else's road.

Read *Build Your Own Road* with an open mind. Try it, you'll like it. It gives a new sense of purpose. It is a great privilege for you to become acquainted with my very good friend and associate.

George H. Oliver
Dean
School of Business
Harding University

Contents

Overview

Life is like a road. It can be smooth or rough, straight or crooked, short or long and dull or interesting.

We are like road builders, because we build our own "roads" in life. Our lives are what we make them. Sometimes, we have to change our plans or directions to accommodate various situations that we either can't avoid or we choose to evade. But isn't that like the road builder who designs highways to avoid certain obstacles?

As travelers, we can reach any destination we choose by taking the right roads. But isn't the same true of life? By taking the right "paths," or courses of action, we can reach any vision of success that we might hold.

Many people plod along through life without a plan for success. Or, worse yet, they operate on someone else's plan—then they wonder why it seems so unfulfilling to them. By failing to design their own roads, they are cheating themselves out of much of the joy that life has to offer.

TWO COMPONENTS OF SUCCESS

To achieve a vision of success, whatever it might be, there are only two requirements to fulfill.

1 Define the vision. Without such a vision, you'll have nothing to reach for. Life can become awfully boring when we haven't determined what it takes to motivate us. Defining our own visions of success can make us excited about pursuing them.

2 Design your road. Whatever your vision, there is a way to achieve it. But you'll have to plot the course and build the road leading to it. No one can or will do it for you.

That's the essence of true success. It might seem simple, but it's not necessarily easy. That's one reason the world is full of frustrated people. They either have no vision of success, or they've never taken the time to design roads leading to it.

Yet, every day, we build our roads a little farther in some direction—whatever direction we might happen to be heading. Often, we don't know what direction our road is going. Yet, we keep right on building.

If you don't know where you're going, how do you know you'll want to be there when you arrive? Unfortunately, many people have built roads taking them precisely where they didn't want to be, simply because they never determined where they wanted to go in the first place.

FOLLOWING OTHER PEOPLE'S ROADS

The majority of people allow others to design their roads. They follow paths that are more or less designed by their employers, spouses, friends and, to some extent, their children. Certainly, there's nothing wrong with allowing valued people to have input into the direction of our life roads, provided that we have final approval.

For example, there's nothing wrong with working for someone else, provided that it's the career direction you want to take. But if your job isn't satisfying you, you're probably building the wrong career road. There's nothing wrong with acting to please spouse, friends and children, provided that you, too, derive satisfaction. It's easy to try to be all things to all people—and fail miserably. If your needs and desires rank low on your list of priorities, it's time you turned your road around.

Life is sort of like a game. There's only one life per player. And if, by the end of the game, we haven't experienced sufficient satisfaction and fulfillment that comes with pursuing meaningful ambitions, we lose the game.

You have only one chance at road building. And if you're not building your road toward the destination of your choice, you're playing a losing game. Yet, I've learned from people who have attended my seminars that many of them feel they don't know how to begin building in the direction of their choice.

In the game of road building, there are no "rules," other than being able to live with the choices you make. Naturally, society will see to it that your road takes a dramatic turn if you're caught breaking the law. But if you can live with the consequences, then even crimes are fair game.

Of course, I'm not encouraging you to take up a criminal life. I'm just trying to point out how free you are to choose your destiny. The only rules in this game are up to you.

I've discovered while conducting seminars that most people have dreams and ambitions they'd like to pursue. It's just that they've gotten so "locked-in" to the business of road-building in the wrong direction that they can't seem to change directions. They frequently say they're going to pursue new routes as soon as their bills are paid and their children are grown. But we who know better realize that there will always be bills, and that our children don't ever completely grow up as long as we're alive. These are just convenient excuses to keep building what we have already started.

These people might have good intentions about building their roads in new directions. But good intentions won't get them anywhere. As they say, "the road to hell is paved with good intentions."

If you want your road to go in a different direction from which it is now heading, you will need more than good intentions. First, you will need potential, which, if you're breathing, you already have. Second, you'll need a willingness to consider new possibilities for your life. The fact you're reading this book indicates you have that, too.

The only other thing you will need is a process that will help you plot the course of your future road. And you've got that, too, because it's in the pages that follow.

THIS BOOK WILL HELP YOU MAKE A START

The process detailed in this book reflects my own experience in road building. I became interested in public speaking and seminar conducting during the 19 years I held various positions with the U.S. Department of Defense. I currently have a dozen years experience as a speaker and trainer. In 1984, I founded Wolfe Associates, and became an independent contractor dedicated to enhancing organizational and personal growth within corporations, institutions and various agencies.

I reached my destination by building my own road. This book will tell you how to build yours—and I stress the word, "how." I cannot and will not tell you in what direction to build. That choice is entirely up to you.

Before you can make any choice regarding the direction of your road, it's important to determine who you are. The first section of the book explores the significance of our self-esteem and how we act consistently with it. It also explains how people often resign themselves to unfavorable circumstances, rather than work to create new ones. Also covered is the concept of a "best self" and how you can develop yours, along with the power of positive thinking and how it can generate a feeling of well-being even on "bad" days.

The second section deals with building your own road. In it, I'll discuss determining your destination—defining success on your own terms—and developing a plan that will help you build your road as you choose. Of course, there are risks with road building, and sometimes, you'll make mistakes that can set you back. I'll explain how risks are necessary for progress, and how mistakes often are our best teachers. I'll discuss the importance of having role models and how they can help us build our roads. There is also a chapter on the magic that results from the pursuit of self-defined success and how this magic can make us happier with our lives. The section concludes with a chapter explaining why road building is never finished, and why we should continue building our roads in our chosen directions.

The final section of the book deals with leadership—the disciplines necessary to keep us building our roads and to help us lead others as they build theirs.

No matter what you do in life, you will build your own road. Whether it goes in the direction you would like depends on whether or not you are in charge of its construction. If you feel like you aren't, or that you could at least be in more control than you already are, then this might be one of the most important books you'll ever read.

Why not get started now? Your road won't wait.

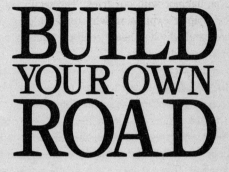

BUILD
YOUR OWN
ROAD

I

DETERMINING WHO YOU ARE

1

Self-Esteem—The Key
to Your Past and Future

If you don't matter to you, it's hard to matter to others.

—MALCOLM FORBES

No matter who you are and what you have done in life, you have been traveling a road that you've built. Perhaps you're already aware of this. And, then, perhaps you're not.

This book is about building roads, and I'm going to tell you how it's done. But first, it's important that you realize that the road you have traveled to this point in life has been of your own making. Whether you're pleased with your life, but would like more than you've been getting, or are outright unhappy with your past, the road you traveled was yours. No one has forced you to travel it, and no one can force you to travel a road you do not want to take. It's vitally important that you understand this, because once you've accepted this concept, then you also can accept the responsibility for changing your direction.

For example, if you quit high school in your teen years,

you chose that road. If you graduated and went to college, you chose your road. If you got married and had children, you chose your road. If you never married, or got a divorce, you still chose your road. If you've been successful in your career, it's because you chose the right road. If you failed, it's possibly because you've chosen the wrong road.

Of course, I understand that some events present themselves which, more or less, dictate the course of our lives. For example, during the 1960's, many young men were conscripted into the armed forces to fight in the Vietnam conflict. A young soldier of that era might argue that his road was chosen for him by the powers that be—the U. S. government. To a point, this might be true. Yet, each and every young man still had the right and privilege to choose his own road—either to comply with the draft, seek refuge in Canada or go to prison. Three different roads diverged for those young men. Each took the road he chose, whether it was selected as the most attractive option or the least unpleasant alternative, as he perceived it.

Others might argue that roads can be dictated for them by other people. The last son or daughter to leave home might feel pressured to remain to care for aging parents. Yet, the offspring has the right to choose his or her own destiny—to stay or remain, depending on which option is perceived to be the most pleasant.

WE CHOOSE THE ROADS WE WANT

Bearing this in mind, I'd like to point out that all of us choose the roads we want in life. Sometimes, our choices might be tough—whether to go on a vacation or stay home to see a visiting relative we haven't seen in five years and, if we don't stay home, won't see for another five. But we choose the road we want to take. It's not a question of whether we're selfish or unselfish, because there's no such thing as being selfish when it comes to doing what we want. You might say that—given the previous option—you might stay home to visit the relative because you wouldn't want to deal with the fallout from other relatives who might criticize you had you gone on the vacation. Even so, you opted for the situation that would cause you the least pain and, as a result, the most pleasure. We choose whatever roads we take because they seem to be the most attractive option at the time.

So why do we choose certain roads over others? Why would one person go to Vietnam, while another went to Canada and still another goes to prison? Why would one person opt to live at home to care for aging parents when another wouldn't even consider the thought? Why would one individual go on a vacation while another would stay home to visit Uncle Bob and Aunt Alice?

The answer to this question will explain why you've traveled the road you've chosen in life. But most importantly, it will determine the future course of your current road. Your road isn't built for you upon your birth. It's not a predestined path that's absolutely unavoidable.

We build our own roads, every day of our lives. And we build them consistent with our self-esteem.

YOUR SELF-ESTEEM IS YOUR "BLUEPRINT"

We form opinions of other people as we meet them, and these opinions are strong factors for how we relate to others. If we think of someone as being friendly and open, we'll most likely be friendly and open with them. If we consider someone cold and aloof, we'll probably give them the same treatment.

Sometimes, these opinions might be wrong. But we still act on them. Many times, we may think of someone as being cold and aloof, and we treat them so, only to change our opinion later as we get to know the person better. Then we change the way we treat them. In other words, opinions may or may not be accurate, but we'll act on them anyway.

So what's your opinion of yourself? Whatever it is, that's your self-esteem. We form our self-esteem based on all the opinions we have of ourselves. And, like we do with others, we treat ourselves—and build our roads—on that basis.

If we see ourselves, for example, as incapable of living a productive existence, we might build for ourselves the roads of criminals or derelicts. But if we see ourselves as productive and responsible, we'll build for ourselves the roads of successful people.

But those are generalized statements. Actually, self-esteem plays an important role in every action we take. Even if we are responsible and productive, we might fear venturing out in new social situations if we see ourselves as socially inept. Or we might be near the top on a wide variety of social invitation lists, yet live the lives of personas non grata (unwelcome people) at home because we don't see ourselves as family oriented.

People act consistently with their self-esteem. That's the way it has been, and that's the way it always will be. If the road that's behind you has caused you pain and remorse, look to your self-esteem for the reason.

But now for the good news. If you don't like the road you've built for yourself, you can change it, because self-esteem is not inherited. It is self-created, which means it can be changed.

As I look back I recognize that I, too, suffered from a low self-esteem. It was similar to being imprisoned. Whenever I thought I might like to do something, make a change in my life, job, appearance, buy a new car, change the wallpaper, I would ponder over "what would others think?" These others included my dad, mom, spouse, neighbors, friends, associates and people I never even met. It was enough to scare the thought right out of me—the fear—the risk—low self-esteem in action.

I was trapped with the question, "Would they like me, would they respect me, would they hate me . . ." Then, "What if I fail, what if I succeed, what if I . . ."

The road of low self-esteem is a deadly road. I chose to get off of that road by changing my attitude. Now I know that:

- It doesn't matter if others see you as a success or failure; what matters is how you see yourself, how you view each success and challenge and what you learn from the experience.

- It makes no difference how much others love you if you do not love yourself.

- It's not what others think of you; it's what you think of you.

- It makes no difference whether or not others respect you if you don't respect you.

- It doesn't matter whether or not others like you if you do not like yourself.

- If you hate yourself, it makes no difference that others hate you, too.

All of us have a choice—the choice to imprison ourselves or the choice to be our own best self. Consider the idea that if we are our own judge, jury, guard at the prison gate and our own prisoner and the warden, then we also hold the power to determine the amount of freedom we have at this very moment.

The key to freedom is our own well developed and defined level of self-esteem. Freedom begins with you. Freedom begins with love of self, commitment and sustained interest in building your own road.

The building of your road starts when you:

- Know that you know

- Take action and make choices

- Stop value judging yourself and others

- Know your developed areas

- Respect yourself as a person of true value

- Know that each day brings many successes

- Love yourself

- Give genuine love to others

- Forgive yourself and others

- Live, laugh, learn, love and listen

SELF-TALK BUILDS SELF-ESTEEM

All of us talk to ourselves. It's only when we talk to ourselves out loud that other people start to wonder about us. When it's done through thought, our self-esteem is affected.

If our opinions of ourselves comprise our self-esteem, then our self-talk is nothing more than opinions of our individual actions and behaviors which, taken collectively, influence our self-esteem.

Self-talk starts early in life, and is in full swing by the time we're in our teens. Our self-talk is what talks us either into or out of doing what we want to do. For example, a teen-ager wants to ask someone out for a date. Yet, the teen is filled with doubts and acknowledges through self-talk that he or she isn't interesting, charming or attractive enough for the other person to accept the invitation. The teen becomes convinced of this, decides not to offer the invitation and develops a devalued self-esteem in the process. Although it might seem juvenile, you and I both know people who subscribe to this type of thinking, even though they are well into adulthood. They are living with the negative or low self-esteem they created years ago.

We can also allow our self-esteem to be adversely affected by negative comments from others. Sometimes, criticism is necessary to maintain a relationship, whether it's socially or career based. But destructive remarks meant to wound more than help can be devaluing to our self-esteem. When we take seriously the negative comments directed to us from someone we perceive as important—whether or not we actually admire them—it's as if we made the negative comment ourselves. For example, we might not like our parents, siblings or co-workers. Yet, we very well might take seriously what they have to say about us because they play significant roles in our lives. If and when you hear negative remarks, consider the source, and be careful how seriously you take the comments. Decide for yourself whether or not they are true.

So if we can create our own negative self-esteem, then doesn't it stand to reason that we can create positive self-esteem, too. You'd better believe we can. In fact, the job is entirely up to the individual. You're the only person who can change your self-esteem for the better.

IT'S ALL IN THE MIND

To better understand how we create our negative and positive self-esteem, let's take a quick look at the human mind. It is divided into left and right hemispheres. The left hemisphere is known to hold the conscious mind. It is in charge of analytical functions such as thinking, speaking, reading, writing, arithmetic, planning, organizing and judgment. The right hemisphere holds the subconscious mind, which provides creativity, sensory information, images, visualization, emotions, intuition and insight. Separating the two hemispheres is a membrane called the corpus callosum, which is responsible for sending messages between the two sides.

The subconscious mind is a storehouse for all the information we've ever learned, be it in the classroom or through actual experience. Of course, everything we learn is experienced first in the conscious mind. From there, it is recorded in the subconscious. Nothing we learn is ever really forgotten. It's all stored in the subconscious mind. Some of it might be effectively "buried" until an occurrence or an event brings it to mind.

For example, a song we sung as children might be seemingly forgotten for years. Then, one day, we hear the song on the radio and, instantly, we find we not only remember the song, but we can recall every word of it. In this case, the song was buried in the subconscious mind until the playing of the song was experienced in the conscious mind. At that point, the corpus callosum sent the message to the subconscious, which responded with the stored information—the music and lyrics.

Now, when we pass either positive or negative judgment on ourselves for an action or behavior, the judgment is first experienced in the conscious mind, then it is relayed to the subconscious mind, where it stays forever. It doesn't matter whether our judgment is accurate or fair. The subconscious mind doesn't make judgments. Remember, that's the job of the conscious mind. It accepts everything as true.

Our subconscious controls our images. And the more we fill it with judgments, the greater those judgments will influence our self-esteem and, as a result, the roads we build.

Simply stated, if we think we're incompetent, we probably will be. But if we think we're responsible and capable, we'll probably possess those traits, too.

So let's put all of this together. We can make our self-esteem to be anything we'd like it to be. And that means that the road ahead of us can go in any direction we'd like—all through the power of self-talk!

PROPS AND CRUTCHES WON'T REPLACE A STRONG SELF-ESTEEM

When people don't feel good about themselves, they often evaluate themselves through "props" and "crutches" that they associate with their self-worth. This is called externalized self-esteem—when an individual's self-worth hinges on possessing certain items or associating with certain people. When I was in school, it used to be called the "in crowd" syndrome.

Too many people don't look within to bolster their self-esteem. Instead, they look outside of themselves. Some people with low self-esteem may find identity through material items. Elegant homes, luxury cars and designer clothes are popular with people who feel the need to affix their identity to objects that can be displayed to all who meet them. (This is not—I repeat *not*—to say that all people with elegant homes, luxury cars or designer clothes operate with weak self-esteem.)

When we're secure with our own identities, we can appreciate the material things of life, because we know we'll still be ourselves, even if we lose them. However, people who are not secure with themselves see the loss of such items as a loss of identity. It's as noted psychologist William James, often referred to as the father of psychology, said: "Lives based on having are less free than lives based either on doing or being."

When we base our self-worth on what we are and what we are capable of doing, then our self-esteem is internalized, or based on our character—the only solid measure of true self-esteem.

People with externalized self-esteem often build roads that reflect an intense pursuit of material items or relationships they perceive will raise their self-esteem. People with internalized self-esteem design their roads to lead to happiness and fulfillment. The friendships and material possessions they accumulate along the way are just "icing on the cake."

WE ALL HAVE VALUE TO OURSELVES

Sometimes, people get their value and their worth mixed up. All people have value, regardless of what they do or who they are. The miracle of birth might be a common miracle, but it's a miracle nonetheless. Each person who has ever lived is a unique being.

An individual's assessment of his or her own value is based on their level of self-esteem. This means that people with low or negative self-esteem perceive themselves as having little if any value. When that's an individual's self-opinion, chances are he or she will have little value. But individual value can be raised by raising self-esteem. Self-esteem increases when we believe—truly believe— we are worthy of our pursuits in life.

Worth is an entirely different matter. Our worth is based on our talents, skills and abilities. Our employers or clients value us to the extent of our contributions to a company, the family, society, a club or church.

Too often, we confuse our worth as perceived by others with our true value. When we do this, our self-esteem becomes externalized. We permit it to rise or fall, depending on what others think about us. The direction of roads built by people who confuse value with worth often is dictated by others. And that's no way for an individual to build a road that he or she, alone, must travel.

Only when we can distinguish between our value and worth can we build roads that will take us where we want to go.

BARRIERS TO ACHIEVEMENT

Roadblocks are frustrating when you're trying to get where you want to go. This is true with actual highways, and it's true for the roads that we build for ourselves. When we can't achieve or attain what we want, we have been effectively delayed by a roadblock.

There are two types of roadblocks that serve as barriers to achievement.

1 Externally imposed. These are factors beyond our control. For example, an individual aspires to a higher position in his or her company, but management decides to fill the vacancy from outside. A runner wants to compete in a marathon, but breaks a leg two weeks before the race. A vacation must be postponed or canceled because a family member becomes too ill to travel. When our plans are ruined by external forces, we can consider these roadblocks that life throws at us, and it's up to us to determine whether to wait for the block to be lifted or to build our road in another direction.

2 Self-imposed. These are factors that are within our control but, for whatever reason, we consciously or subconsciously choose not to control them. For example, we don't finish assigned work on time because we procrastinate. We don't undertake a certain project because we are intimidated by its magnitude. We shy away from new endeavors because we feel we aren't qualified or capable of meeting the challenge. Of course, self-imposed barriers are roadblocks of our own making.

The more self-imposed roadblocks we create, the lower our level of self-esteem. We can't help but deal with the external roadblocks that life or other people throw at us. But life is simply too short to build a road that falls short of our destinations because construction was frequently delayed by self-imposed roadblocks. Whenever we impose roadblocks to our achievement, we restrict our achievement and our enjoyment of life.

Remember that only you can build your road. And remember that no one is better qualified than you to build it.

So before we talk about your future, let's take a look at your current situation—your personal state of affairs, which is the topic of the next chapter.

2

Your State of Affairs

The life of man is a journey; a journey that must be traveled, however bad the roads or the accommodations.
—OLIVER GOLDSMITH

Let's talk about your road, not so much as to how you've built it up to this point, but in what direction you plan to build it from here forward.

How is your life going? If you're like many people, you're probably satisfied with it overall, but there are some parts of it that you feel could stand improvement. Or perhaps you have your eye on interesting areas far away from your current road, which would require construction in a completely different direction. If so, there will never be a better time than now to alter your course.

It bothers me a great deal to meet people at my seminars or speaking engagements who really want to build their roads in different directions, yet feel they are locked into their current courses by circumstances. For example, many people are not happy with their lives because they are unhappy in their jobs. Yet, they feel ''locked-in'' to their jobs by circumstances. Perhaps they have too many debts and obligations to give up a secure position. Maybe they feel they don't have enough experience to seek work in another field. So they continue building a road that leads to an unfulfilling, mundane existence.

Personally, that doesn't make much sense to me. Of course, I can appreciate a person's apprehensions about taking their roads in different, uncertain directions. But if they know their roads are headed for unhappiness, why keep building in the same direction?

It's like a piece of advice I was once given: "When you find that you've dug your way into a hole, stop digging!"

CIRCUMSTANCES GET A RAW DEAL

Too many people blame circumstances for their failures. They cite rules, other people, power games, a lack of control or no available options for their being unsuccessful. But we create many of our own circumstances through our choices. That means we can create new circumstances, if we want, by making new choices.

As noted playwright George Bernard Shaw once said,

"People are always blaming their circumstances for what they are. I don't believe in circumstances. The people who get on in this world are the people who get up and look for the circumstances they want. And if they can't find them, they make them."

We live in a world where a majority of people blame circumstances for their situations and their feelings. Too often, we feel that we must do certain things because they're required of us. We blame other people for our self-developed frenzies and frustrations. Yet, this belief of having no personal control is amazing to me. Regardless of the situation, we do have control over some things. The main thing we have control over is how we react to any given situation.

WE CONTROL OUR ATTITUDES

Some people believe that we can't help how we feel, and to a certain extent, that's true. We don't consciously choose our emotions. But we most certainly can help how we react to an upsetting situation.

I'd like to share with you an event that was devastating to me—the death of my brother, Dennis. He was killed in Vietnam in 1966 at the age of 19.

Dennis never felt he was successful at anything he did in his short life—until he enlisted in the Army. He was amazed that he was accepted. He became private first-class and a sharpshooter, and he apparently was very good at it. He wrote me a letter saying, "I feel so good. I finally found something I can do—something I believe in." Unfortunately, his expert ability and his belief in that ability actually moved him in the direction of his death.

Dennis had not only been my older brother, but he had been my best friend and guardian angel all of my life—especially during the years when we lived in the ghetto. Dealing with his death was not an easy matter, but I was able to come to grips with it by remembering the good times we had and realizing that he died while doing something he felt was best for him at the time. Focusing on that realization was an emotionally cleansing experience for me.

My mother, however, did not quite see it that way. With all due respect, she was frozen in the belief that God and Uncle Sam were responsible for Dennis' death. Nothing could change her mind—not my dad, the priest, the Army or her other five children and two step-children.

It took Mother 22 years to recognize that this was Dennis' choice. He believed in what he was doing and was willing to accept the consequences. Now, all of these years later, my mother is heavily involved in the Gold Star Mothers Organization, which is dedicated to the families who lost loved ones during war. Mother carries the flag, addresses groups, and shares her story. Our family has learned a great deal by addressing her turn to freedom from the past.

My point is this: Look at the negatives in your life and change them into positives. You use the same amount of energy, and life is much more beautiful.

We can't always control what happens to us, but we can always control our reactions to it. It's simply a matter of viewpoint. I believe that no matter how unfortunate, disappointing or devastating our circumstances, we can redirect that energy into creating a positive, success-oriented circumstance in our minds that can help us cope.

For example, Viktor E. Frankl was a German psychologist who was imprisoned in a concentration camp during World War II. In his book, *Man's Search For Meaning*, he points out that prisoners who resisted by lashing out at their captors were killed on the spot. Other prisoners were so overwhelmed by their bleak existence that they gave up the will to live and died. The only prisoners who stood a chance of survival were those who accepted the reality of their situations and devoted their efforts toward helping and comforting others.

If concentration camp prisoners who witnessed mass executions—sometimes of their own family members—could create positive, success-oriented circumstances in such an environment, then can't we, too?

PROBLEMS ARE OPPORTUNITIES

One way we can create success-oriented circumstances in the midst of disappointment or despair is by viewing our problems as opportunities. All problems offer us at least the opportunity to solve them. And every problem has a solution, even if it's only to adopt the right attitude, as was the case with my outlook toward my brother's death.

But many problems offer us more than just an exercise in attitude. For example, if money becomes too tight to maintain our current lifestyle, we have the opportunity to learn to be content with less. In time, this could be a blessing, because we will be better prepared the next time money becomes scarce. If getting a promotion at work hinges on a qualification we don't have, we have the opportunity to develop the qualification through education or actual experience. This could make us better prepared for the promotion or even an entirely new career situation.

No one likes having problems. Yet, that doesn't change the fact that having and solving problems is not only what makes life interesting, but it also helps us develop character, abilities and inner strength. And, what's more, having and solving problems helps us develop directions for the roads we build in life by allowing us to create for ourselves new circumstances.

COMFORT ZONES ARE CONFINING

Many people don't create new situations for themselves because they're too comfortable with their current circumstances. You'll take note that I didn't say they were happy with their circumstances—only comfortable.

We all seek comfort to some degree, and there's nothing wrong with that. But when our lifestyles become so comfortable that we no longer desire to expand our horizons, then they become confining.

We create our own "comfort zones" or lifestyles that aren't quite fulfilling but are too comfortable to give up to seek fulfillment elsewhere. In a sense, our comfort zones become our prisons, because it often takes a lot of courage to break out of them.

Many of my seminar attendees point to their comfort zones as the circumstances that prevent them from being successful. They have become so dependent on the lifestyles they've created that they feel powerless to give them up to seek greener pastures. They blame circumstances which they created and which they can change.

YOUR LIFE IS UNIQUE

As I pointed out in Chapter One, every person in the world is unique; no two are exactly alike, even if they come from identical backgrounds and cultures. This is true partly because no two people are going to experience identical circumstances. Remember, most of our circumstances are self-made.

We become very complex as we move through our lives. Each individual is the result of his or her physical self, personal values, recreational pursuits, social activities, spiritual beliefs, intelligence quotient (IQ), education, personal history, self-image and self-esteem.

Even if two people did have identical qualities, they still wouldn't be identical people. When these qualities are combined through the "funnel of love and life," they are combined in different ways. Life helps us form our attitudes and perceptions through the people we meet, the experiences we have and the lessons we learn.

From this mixture comes a "unique factor," or a common thread that takes us from our beginnings to our current and future selves. This factor reflects our attitudes and perceptions, our actions and reactions to life, our motivation or lack of motivation.

One of the most important issues of the unique factor is choice. Our lives are the result of our choices. We choose to be who we are, what we are and what we do. The differences between people lies in the different choices they make. When we feel powerless to make a choice, we do not have control of our lives. And if we lack control of our lives, then we can neither define nor design our own success.

When it comes to building our own roads, if we can't choose, we lose.

LIFE IS A MARATHON

When you really think about it, life is one big marathon.

Let me explain. An actual marathon is a race involving a route that runs slightly more than 26 miles. Hundreds if not thousands of people enter the well known marathons. A few of the contestants run a marathon to win. They are striving to finish first. Most of the other entrants only desire to complete the race and, hopefully, set a new personal record in the process. These people aren't in competition with anyone except themselves. And then, there are some contestants who start out gung-ho, only to fall by the wayside when the run becomes too uncomfortable for them to continue.

Isn't that the way life is? Some people live it as if it were a race that they must win. Others live life to make increasingly impressive personal achievements, but they don't feel the need to be "king of the mountain." Still others can't inconvenience themselves long enough to suit up for the game.

If we choose to run the marathon, regardless of the reason, then there are certain characteristics we must develop. And the same is true for people who would lead fulfilling lives. Let's take a look at these characteristics.

1 Self-motivation. Whether we're running a marathon or building our own roads, we must be self-motivated. We can't wait for external circumstances to provide us with the incentive to achieve. We must create circumstances that will motivate us to act.

2 Dedication. People don't complete marathons—let alone win them—without being dedicated. Running 26 plus miles is not an endeavor for on-again, off-again runners. Likewise, building a road leading to a fulfilling existence requires dedication. It's hard work, coupled with the reward of achievement, that makes life interesting.

3 Faith. Belief is essential for running a marathon or building a road. Marathoners don't compete in races they don't think they can win or complete. As road builders, we can't build roads we don't believe we can travel. Faith is a requirement for success of any kind, and the person who tries to run a race or build a road without faith probably won't be satisfied with the results.

4 Preparation. A marathon places physical, mental and emotional demands upon the runner. When the starting gun fires, the runner had better be prepared. Life also places demands on us—physical, mental, emotional and, sometimes, financial. When we're building our roads, we'd better be prepared to meet those demands, lest we be forced to detour or be delayed by a roadblock.

5 Awareness. Marathon runners must be aware of all opportunities and enter the race that they believe to be the best option for them at the time. They don't run the race that others want them to run; they depend on their own judgment, and they choose their contests based upon what they know about themselves and their abilities. Road builders also must be aware of their environments. They must scan the universe for the best opportunities to suit their talents, skills, abilities and their desires.

6 Enjoyment of effort. Marathoners must plan for the future, but they must not lose sight of the present and forget to enjoy the run. When we build our roads, we must focus on our destinations, but not to the point that we forget to enjoy the construction itself. To achieve what we want, we must enjoy the total effort, from conception to completion. Then, we'll be able to look back on the experience with fond memories, a sense of pride, a sense of humor and, above all, a sense of accomplishment and worth.

7 Vision of victory. Some marathoners are running to win, while others run to participate and complete the race. Each runner decides what he or she wants, then expends the effort to achieve it. The sense of worth that comes with achievement is based on the choices we make in the beginning. We decide where we want our roads to go, then we build them in that direction. It makes no difference what direction our neighbor's roads are going, or the direction that our parents' roads went. We create our own victories by determining the course of our roads. As a result, we become the architects of our own lives.

8 Pacing. Pacing is important to marathon runners. There's no point in starting out full speed ahead, leaving all opponents at the starting line, only to collapse from exhaustion a half-mile into the race. Pacing is absolutely essential for road builders. Remember, it's important to enjoy the effort, and we can't enjoy building our roads if we're in a hurry to finish. Also, if we don't pace ourselves, we, like marathoners, might collapse before we reach our destinations.

9 Commitment. Marathoners commit themselves to finishing the race. Despite the pain and fatigue they experience, they condition themselves to run to the finish line. People who build roads leading to fulfilling destinations commit themselves to completing them. They make the decision to stay in for the long haul.

Marathoners don't have to run. No one places a gun to their heads. They run because they want to run. We do what we want to do in life; no one forces us to do it.

Sometimes, people will say to me, "It looks like you're working too hard." But I want to work hard, because I enjoy what I do. Yet, when I watch marathon runners in a race, I'll catch myself saying, "These people are killing themselves. Why are they working so hard?"

Of course, the answer is the same. They want to work hard. They, like myself, could quit anytime they wanted to do something else. But they don't want to quit, and neither do I.

I've had marathon contestants tell me that sometimes they hate running because it makes their lungs burn and their feet ache. It aggravates their shin splints, gives them a pounding headache and makes them feel nauseated. So

I've told them to sit down and take it easy. They don't have to run. No one is making them.

And they respond by saying, "If I don't run, I won't win the race." We all make our choices.

What is it you really want? What's your quest in life? Where do you put your commitment and dedication? And what are you willing to put on the line for it? It's difficult to make significant achievements and leave our comfort zones intact. Marathoners willingly make the necessary sacrifices, and so do road builders who are headed for an exciting destination.

And I hope you will, too. We all live the lives we choose, but only a few of us will live self-designed lives. It's a challenging quest for anyone who is willing to meet the demands. The bottom line is securing the real, evasive happiness and personal satisfaction that life gladly gives to those who are willing to work for it.

No matter what road you aspire to build, you'll do the best job if you are the best "you" possible. So let's move on to the next chapter, where I'll explain how to build your best self.

3

Building a Better Self

The hardest victory is the victory over self.
—ARISTOTLE

Are you the best "you" there is? If you're not, you're doing yourself and those who depend on you a disservice.

You are a unique being, the genetic result of your ancestral past. And if you want to know how unique you are, consider that you have two parents, four grandparents, eight great-grandparents, 16 great-great grandparents and 32 great-great-great-grandparents. Of course, we could go on and on, since the number doubles for each removed generation. But each of these people played an important part in bringing you to reality. Had just one of them decided to marry and have children with someone else, you never would have existed!

So I hope you can see that you are quite unique. After all, there was only one combination of people over centuries of time that could have led to your existence, and the fact that you're reading this book shows that it occurred without a hitch.

So now that you're here at long last, what do you plan to do to make the time you live worthwhile? How are you spending your proverbial "three score and ten"?

Sadly, I know people whose lives consist of nothing but working at unfulfilling jobs by day and watching television shows by night. When it comes to building roads, they've effectively reached dead ends.

Yet, I know many other people who give meaning to their existence by subjecting themselves to new experiences on all of life's levels. They seek and obtain fulfilling jobs, meaningful relationships, solid educations, stimulating recreational pursuits and rewarding social activities. When it comes to building roads, they have constructed smooth thoroughfares with clearly established exit and return access ramps leading to and from a variety of pursuits. Their lives are interesting and worthwhile.

Which type of person are you? The answer to that question isn't nearly as important as the answer to the next question: Which type of person do you want to be? You can be any type of person you'd like, provided you're willing to build the road that will take you there.

HOW YOU GOT TO WHERE YOU ARE TODAY

Your ancestors are responsible for your arrival on earth. But you are responsible for what you have become since then. I offered the "funnel of love and life" in the previous chapter as an explanation of how we develop into the unique human beings that we are. But let's take a closer look at the process to give you a better understanding of how you have determined your own development.

1 **Physical self.** Up to a point, your body is the result of your ancestors at work. If you were blessed with a

sound mind and body, credit it to your ancestors. This accomplishment was pretty much out of your hands. However, what becomes of our bodies as we mature falls into the area of our responsibility. Barring accidents or illnesses, if our adult bodies are in good shape, we can take the credit. If not, only we can take the blame.

2 Values. We learn much of our values as children. We listen and often echo the opinions of our parents and valued peers. Even so, as we mature, we might adapt or revise values we learned as children to better suit our situations and our beliefs.

3 Recreation. The things we do for fun are likely to be influenced by our families when we're young. As we grow and meet others, we develop our own tastes for recreation that might, though not necessarily, parallel those of our parents.

4 Social activities. This area often reflects choices based on everything from an individual's free will to peer pressure. And peer pressure is strong motivation for anyone of any age. People who build their own roads aren't influenced by the crowd; instead, they participate in the social activities that most appeal to them.

5 Spiritual beliefs. This is another category that is heavily influenced by our parents when we are young. Yet, it's not at all unusual for us to develop our own religious preferences and spiritual beliefs when we become adults and are more prone to think for ourselves.

6 Intelligence Quotient. There are two schools of thought on how we develop our IQ's. Some experts believe intelligence is a matter of heredity. Others point to individual attitudes and self-esteem as the determining factors. My advice is simple. Don't worry about your IQ. Simply act intelligently, which is done by making decisions based on all available facts.

7 Education. Obviously, your education will have a strong impact on who you are and what you do. If you don't like the direction of your current road, perhaps you can change it with additional education. People interested in building the best of all possible roads realize that education is a life-long experience.

8 Experiences/history. We grow as the result of education, whether it's obtained in the classroom or through life experiences. Sometimes, the best lessons are the hardest to learn, because they cause us pain. The road behind us reflects our past experiences. All of our experiences offer us benefits. If nothing else, they can help us build better roads in the future since we can learn from our mistakes.

Take a few minutes to reflect on your own past road by examining these qualities in yourself. If you're not happy with the direction of your road, perhaps you can find the trouble spots in one or more of these characteristics. Your past can be helpful when you learn from it.

ARE YOU YOUR "BEST" SELF?

If I were to ask "Who are you?" how would you answer?

Many people would begin by giving their names, quite

naturally. But if pressed for more specific information, they might reveal their occupations, their marital status and, if applicable, the names of their spouses and children. Pressed even further, they might go on to reveal their hobbies and favorite pastimes. Pressed still further, they might even share their dreams for the future.

But none of these explanations would suffice as a suitable response for "Who are you?" They would be excellent responses if we were to be asked what we do or what we want to become. The many roles we play in life—spouse, parent, career person, etc.—fall under the category of the things we do or aspire to do in life.

Who are you? I've discovered during the personal improvement seminars I conduct that many of the participants have a difficult time answering this question. They are so caught up in the roles they play that they don't have time to stop to think about who they are.

Who are you? Before you even consider building any more of your road, I would advise you to ponder this question long and hard. It's the only way to be sure that the road you build is heading in the direction you want it to go.

Let me give you some food for thought on this issue. Who we are is separate from what we do. The roles we play can and often do end long before our lives are over. While we might be parents for the rest of our lives, the role becomes virtually inactive when our children become responsible (or old enough to think they are responsible, whichever comes first). Many of us might want to keep working for the rest of our lives. But if we're employed by a company with a mandatory retirement-age policy, we might be forced to forfeit our roles as employees before we're ready. It might seem that declaring our interest in a particular hobby would be a reflection of who we are. But we might be forced to abandon certain hobbies when conditions are no longer favorable to pursuing them. For example, an avid needlepoint artist afflicted with arthritis might discover that what once was a pleasant hobby has become a frustrating, painful chore. Or a single person with a penchant for racing motorcycles might find it necessary to settle for a less exciting—and decidedly safer—way to spend free time should he or she decide to raise a family.

None of what we do should be confused with who we are. The various roles we play in life can be abdicated or even eliminated. But we are who we are for as long as we live.

We need to be aware of, and believe in, our "best" selves, which is who we are, separate and apart from our various life roles. Sooner or later, we all face the loss of some of our roles. If we lose sight of who we are, the loss of a role can be traumatic. But when we remain focused on our best selves, we'll be in shape to recover and even grow from the loss by redirecting our talents and energies in another direction. For example, a marathon runner who suddenly becomes crippled might become a coach and play a significant role in helping other runners succeed.

BUILDING OUR BEST SELVES

By now, you are probably wondering, "What is my best self?" That's a good question. Yet, there is no one more qualified than you to answer it. I can, however, give you a general guideline to follow.

Human beings consist of three elements—mind, body and soul. You can develop your best self by raising your physical, mental and emotional states to top form. Here are a few ways you can do this.

Exercise Regularly

Many people think exercise benefits only the physical self. While there is no denying that exercise makes us physically fit, it also offers rich benefits for our mental and emotional states.

When we exercise, we strengthen our cardiovascular systems, burn off excess calories and, depending on the activity, possibly build muscle. At the same time, the activity also stimulates our brains, which secrete endorphins—a natural chemical that can produce a natural high and a feeling of well-being. Believe me, it would take a lot of effort to maintain a mentally or emotionally depressed state after a vigorous exercise session.

Health experts advise that three 20- to 30-minute exercise sessions per week can go a long way toward developing your best self. As for the type of exercise, that's entirely up to you. But let me give you two pieces of advice.

First, your chosen form of exercise must be fun if you want to maintain it indefinitely. For example, if you hate to jog, I wouldn't advise taking it up, because you probably won't keep it up long (unless you learn to like it). There are all kinds of alternative exercises, including swimming, biking, dancing or weight-lifting, just to name a few.

Also, if you're extremely out of shape, I would suggest walking. Some experts say that it takes just as many calories to walk a mile as it does to run a mile; the jogger might be exercising more intensely, but the pedestrian is exercising for a longer period of time. Thus, the calories burned for any given distance tend to be the same. Also, walking doesn't offer the physical wear and tear that runners frequently experience.

Stick to a Sensible Diet

The food we eat is fuel to keep our bodies functioning. If we fill our bodies with junk foods, we won't function as efficiently as will people who eat sensibly from the four food groups—meat, fish and poultry; fruits and vegetables; whole grains; and dairy products.

In addition to exercising, diet is vital to building your best self. And the term ''diet'' is not to be confused with ''crash'' or ''fad'' diets. Avoid these diets like the plague. Any regimen that dramatically limits your caloric intake will automatically lower your metabolism, which is the rate your body burns calories. Such regimens not only defeat their purposes, but they can actually can be harmful because much of the weight loss comes from muscle instead of fat. Also, when you abandon the crash diet and resume your accustomed caloric intake, your metabolism will remain unchanged, which means you'll gain back all your lost weight, and more.

The only sure way to lose weight and keep it off is through a combination of exercise and sensible diet, which often means establishing new eating habits. It will take longer to produce results, but the results you do produce will make it worth your effort.

Keep Your Stress Level Low

Too much stress can hit us where we live—physically, mentally and emotionally. A certain amount of pressure can help us perform to our potential. That's good, healthy stress. But too much stress is distress, and it can be crippling. Of course, being in good health can help us better withstand distress, and that's where exercise and proper diet come into play. The human brain does a great deal to take care of us without voluntary effort on our parts.

For example, you've probably heard of the "fight or flight" syndrome. When faced with a threatening situation, the brain automatically increases its secretion of adrenaline. Our muscles tighten, increased sugar is deposited in the blood and our breathing becomes rapid and shallow, giving us the energy either to fight or flee, whichever is appropriate. After using this increased energy, the body resumes its natural state. This natural defense mechanism came in handy when our ancestors were blazing trails in the lawless wild while coping with attacks from ferocious animals or other people.

Ironically, it's this same fight or flight syndrome that creates our distress in modern times. Although we might not frequently face physical danger, we do find ourselves in emotionally taxing situations where neither physical combat nor fleeing is considered appropriate. A difficult child, an unreasonable supervisor or betrayal by a close friend or lover can trigger this involuntary response. When the "fight or flight" energy is not released, extreme frustration results from the taxing physical changes, which leads to distress. Uncontrolled stress and fatigue can ruin our health. Ultimately, it can lead to fatal heart attacks and strokes.

Fortunately, there is a way we can deal with the fight or flight syndrome without resorting to fighting or running. One solution is extremely simple—practicing deep breathing from the diaphragm.

Many people breath incorrectly. They expand their chests and pull in their stomachs when breathing. This method might produce an impressive appearance for a member of the armed services, but it's an extremely inefficient way to administer oxygen to our bodies. Chest-breathers take up to 20 shallow breaths per minute. But when we take deep breaths from the diaphragm, or the muscular partition separating the abdomen from the chest, we thrust out our abdomens, which allows our lungs to inflate fully. Diaphragmatic breathers can take as little as six breaths per minute, yet still take in more oxygen than the average chest-breather. This increased oxygen signals to our brains that the situation is under control, and our bodies return to their normal states.

Laughter is one of the most healing activities I have ever experienced. I discovered this early in my life. The ability to laugh at yourself and your situations is a prescription for sanity. In my town of Plymouth, Michigan, we are known for the many trains that travel through our area. When I first moved to Plymouth, I noticed irate behavior on the part of the drivers waiting for the tracks to be cleared. For the most part, waiting does not bother me, and I use the time to do nothing, sing along to my favorite country music or conduct my favorite symphony. I am known for wearing a spongy red clown nose to relieve tension. I put it on while waiting for trains, on airplanes when the passengers get impatient and even in restaurants when I am not getting the attention I need from the server. It works every time, and it lightens my day and often brings a smile to other people, too.

I have given noses to many people, including my husband Michael. Sometimes, even the best communication can get bogged down due to fatigue and everyday living. When that happens with Michael and me, it's "nose time." We are convinced that two people wearing red noses, grinning from the sight, cannot remain angry with each other. "Nose Time" is a lot better than "Miller Time." The tension eases and then we can truly communicate with each other.

In the seminars I conduct, I always ensure that humor is a part of the day. Humor, when used in a positive way, demonstrates control of the situation, opens the avenues for self-awareness, provides a sense of peacefulness, calmness and learning.

From a physiological standpoint, when you laugh, certain hormones trigger the release of endorphins. Endorphins are the body's natural painkillers. When you laugh, your muscles actually vibrate and are considered to provide an internal massage, breaking up the tension. Also, the heart rate and rate of blood circulation levels change to rates similar to a cardiovascular workout, such as fast walking and aerobics.

Now I'm not saying we can solve all of life's problems by deep breathing and laughter. I'm simply saying that deep breathing and laughter can eliminate the distress that prevents us from being our best selves, which is exactly what we need to be when overcoming the roadblocks that life all too often presents.

Watch Your Habits

Exercise, proper diet and stress control go a long way toward helping us develop our best selves. Beyond that, the rest of building our best selves is up to us. We can strengthen or cripple our best selves through our good and bad habits.

If our bodies will function no better than the nutrients we put into them, then it only stands to reason that our brains will function no better than the behavior we program them to output.

Virtually everything we do is a matter of mind programming. Our brains are powerful computers. Everything we learn is stored in our subconscious mind. When we consciously decide to do something that we've already learned how to do, our actions are, more or less, automatic. For example, we consciously decide to take a walk, tie our shoes or drive a car. But we can do these things while consciously concentrating on something else, all because the "how-to" knowledge is stored in our subconscious minds.

It's the same way with our habits. Any action repeated frequently will become habit, and it will remain habit until the mind is reprogrammed to eliminate the habit. And all of our habits are either beneficial, neutral or detrimental to our physical, mental or emotional states.

For example, exercise can become a habit that can benefit us physically, while excessive smoking or drinking can be physically detrimental. Positive thinking can benefit our mental states, while negative thinking can offer adverse affects. Practicing good time management can make us more productive and, thus, offer positive effects to our emotional states, while chronic procrastination can have the reverse effect.

Be careful about the habits you form. If they aren't helping you in the construction of your road, you might consider replacing them with more productive habits.

And don't be afraid to kick unproductive or harmful habits. Sure, it might be tough. But it can be done. The first requirement is having the proper attitude. That's the subject of the next chapter.

4

Yes, You Can;
No Matter What Happens

Happiness and success in life do not depend upon our circumstances but on ourselves.

—SIR JOHN LUBBOCK

Have you ever had days when you felt like dirt, and that everything you touched turned to dirt? If so, relax. You're human.

Still, days like that sting when they pop up from time to time. And when you feel like your day's effort is mediocre at best, it's really easy to let your self-esteem slide.

Only God in His infinite wisdom knows why we have days like this. If I had to venture a guess, I would say they exist so we can develop a greater appreciation of our good days.

I'm sure you've had rough days. I know I have. Furthermore, you and I both will continue to have some "dirt days" from now on. The number of dirt days and the degree to which we allow dirt days to affect our lives is strictly under our control.

But do we have to let our self-esteem slide when we

have them? Absolutely not! Just because we have rotten days doesn't mean we can't feel good about ourselves. There are at least four benefits to feeling right when things go wrong:

1 We stand a greater chance of correcting our mistakes and being in top form to meet the rest of the day's demands.

2 Even if our day doesn't improve, feeling good still beats feeling like dirt.

3 Even if the day actually gets worse, feeling good about ourselves will help us avoid taking out our frustrations on our co-workers and winding up as the subject of an impromptu lunch-hour roast.

4 We may be able to laugh at the chain of events and ourselves—if not today, then tomorrow. Laughter always makes us feel better.

It all goes back to the issue we raised in Chapter Two. We can't always control what happens to us, but we can always control our reaction to what happens.

Happiness doesn't depend on our circumstances. It's a state of mind that we can develop and maintain, regardless of circumstances. True, some circumstances might be more conducive to happiness than others. I would find it easier to be happy vacationing at some remote, idyllic hideaway with my husband than I would to be happy while having my wisdom teeth extracted. But the fact still remains that attitude is the key.

So how can we be happy on dirt days? One good way

I've found to keep my spirits high when my personal effectiveness is low is to remember good days of the past—days when I sparkled in the spotlight of recognition and admiration.

WHAT'S IN THE BASKET?

Yes, I've had dirt days, but I've had my share of good days, too, and so have you. I'll not bore you with a list of Lois Wolfe-Morgan's good days, but I would like to share one particular day in my past that helps brighten the present when the proverbial dark clouds materialize.

When I was in the fourth grade, Detroit's St. Elizabeth High School was staging a Christmas production which offered a part for one child. Out of the dozens of children who auditioned for the part, I was the one who was chosen. Now I know that probably doesn't seem like a big deal to you, but put yourself in the place of a nine-year-old child who suddenly became popular with a score of teen-agers who thought she was adorable. That's how I felt. I rehearsed with my older friends for about six weeks to prepare for the show. Let me tell you, my self-esteem didn't suffer one bit from that experience.

I had a very small part—one line, to be exact—and my appearance was saved for the final scene of the show. Without getting into the details of the plot, I played the role of an angel. Dressed in a pink, satin "angel" gown, I made my entrance concealed in a basket, which was carried on stage by two of the other characters. When the question was asked, "What's in the basket?" that was my cue to jump up like a jack-in-the-box and proclaim, "I am in the basket!"

Of course, I had great fun throughout the rehearsal period. And, as fate would have it, when it was time for the actual performance, my paper halo was knocked askew when I jumped up and knocked the lid off the basket. But the audience didn't seem to mind, judging by their laughter and applause. Like a trouper, I simply raised my halo and went on with my line—"I am in the basket!"

STRAIGHTEN YOUR HALO

All too often in life, it's easy to feel like our "haloes," so to speak, have been tarnished or knocked off-center. But let's acknowledge reality. No one can do anything to your personal halo—unless you let them. Your boss can chew you out, your associates can laugh at you to your face and your spouse or significant other can give you the cold shoulder. But none of them can touch your halo, or your self-esteem. If it slides, it's because you let it slide.

And it's also important to remember that if your halo does fall, it's not necessary to leave it on the ground. You can pick it up and put it back on anytime you are ready.

That's the lesson I learned in retrospect from my experience in the basket. And now, decades later, whenever I have a dirt day and I feel my halo start to lose some of its luster, I simply recall the day when that proud nine-year-old girl simply righted her lopsided halo and proclaimed, "I am in the basket!"

Life is too short to be down on yourself, even for a day. I know it's tough to pull yourself up when circumstances seem to be pushing you down. But you can help pick yourself back up by recalling some golden memory of your past when you were in top form.

Why not make a list of your past successes and pleasant moments in life? Just the memory of them can help you laugh, raise your spirits and elevate your self-esteem at times when they badly need lifting. As a result, you might very well be able to turn what began as a bad day into what may become another golden memory.

I know it can be a real challenge. Just remember what President Abraham Lincoln once said: ''People are just about as happy as they make up their minds to be.'' So when things get rough, you have a choice. You can be happy or unhappy. If being unhappy could change your circumstances for the better, then I would be the first to recommend indulgence in self-pity and sorrow.

Since it won't, why not be happy? It might not solve your problems or eliminate your troubles. But it might help ward off additional woes before they have the chance to materialize. In my opinion, that makes happiness pretty powerful stuff. And it's far cheaper than anything you'll find in a liquor store.

KEEP GOOD COMPANY

If happiness is a matter of attitude, then what determines our attitudes? Clearly, it's a matter of personal choice. We choose our viewpoints. For example, a soaking rainstorm might be perceived as disappointing to the family that had planned a picnic. But to the farmer whose crops are on the verge of wilting, the rainstorm is a godsend.

Attitudes result from our thoughts. Many situations can be viewed as pleasant or unpleasant. A promotion at work means more authority; it usually means more work, too. A family vacation might mean a break from routine; it also might mean spending 24 hours a day with screaming children and a barking dog. A new friendship might mean pleasant companionship; it also might mean hurt feelings if the friendship doesn't work out.

Each situation can be good or bad, depending on how we view it. Our views come from our thoughts, and our thoughts are heavily influenced by our choice of friends and associates. If you run with a crowd that thrives on summer activity, you might be depressed when autumn rolls around. On the other hand, if your crowd lives for the football season, autumn might be your favorite time of year.

Perhaps the greatest influence our friends and associates have on us is not so much in their personal likes and dislikes, but in the general tone of their thinking. Are they positive people, or are they negative? Positive people see the silver linings in dark clouds; negative people see only the clouds.

I know someone who is a very negative person. One day, I became so frustrated with her negative attitude that I just had to ask, "What makes you so negative?" I really didn't expect an answer, but I got one. The woman replied, "When I'm negative, I get more attention."

I guess she's right. Personally, I can live without that kind of attention, and I can definitely live without the kind of company that negative people provide. Attitudes are contagious, and if we associate primarily with negative people, we'll find ourselves thinking negatively.

Positive attitudes also are contagious. If we associate primarily with positive people, we'll find ourselves thinking positively. And that's a clear advantage in any endeavor we would undertake.

When looking toward the future, negative people often foresee gloom and doom. Positive people are different. They don't wear rose-colored glasses, but they never lose sight of hope. The future always holds hope, and it's that very hope that motivates positive people to productive activity.

I've always loved the story of "The Little Steam Engine That Could." You're probably familiar with it. A little steam engine was convinced it wouldn't be able to climb a steep hill. "I think I can't," the little engine at first told itself. But the engine took the advice of a more experienced model—to think positively. "I think I can," the little engine told itself. And it did.

I'm not telling you who to associate with. I'm not even saying that you can't have negative friends (although I wouldn't want one for a roommate or, God forbid, a spouse). But I am saying that the more positive friendships we cultivate, the better off we'll be in developing our own positive attitude.

THE "POOR LITTLE ME" SYNDROME

Even worse than a negative attitude is the "poor little me" syndrome. A person afflicted with a case of this is looking for a savior, and the would-be rescuer who would answer the call will deserve everything he or she gets.

(To quote an old maxim, "No good deed shall go unpunished.")

Linda (not her real name) was a friend of mine who experienced a series of utterly terrible tragedies. I won't deny that her spirit was shattered, and it had good reason to be. At 22, life was going well for her. She had a good job, a precious godchild (who also was her first cousin) and she was engaged to be married.

Suddenly, her life went dramatically downhill with a series of events that would seem difficult to believe even in a soap opera. Her fiance, along with three mutual friends, was killed in a car wreck. That's enough to break anyone's heart. But that's just the tip of the iceberg.

With her fiance recently buried, Linda's favorite aunt dropped dead of a brain aneurism at the age of 32, leaving behind three children—the youngest of whom was Linda's godchild. The child's father subsequently moved his family to the East coast for what he thought would be a healing change of scenery.

But it wasn't long before tragedy struck again. The godchild was struck by an automobile and killed. By this time, the child's father had reached his emotional limit. Just prior to the child's funeral, he hanged himself in the basement of the church.

At this point, Linda was feeling pretty wretched about life. But her troubles weren't over. Shortly after her uncle's death, Linda's mother and father announced their plans to divorce. Next, Linda contracted a case of breast cancer, which put her in the hospital for surgery and a series of chemotherapy treatments.

Upon her recovery, Linda immediately became involved with the type of guy that no woman should ever get involved with. She became pregnant and, naturally, the guy disappeared. Linda decided on abortion. Throughout this stressful existence, Linda's job performance suffered, and she ultimately was given a reprimand. (Talk about adding insult to injury!)

THE LOSS OF OUR ROLES

In Chapter Three, we talked about how people sometimes confuse their actual value with their worth, which often can be found in the roles they play in life. When those roles are lost, people with low self-esteem tend to devalue themselves.

So let's recap Linda's lost roles and illustrate how they affected her. The car wreck cost not only her status as a fiance, but it also eliminated a large part of her social circle with the three friends who also died. She lost her position as a niece with the death of her aunt, and she lost her status as a godmother when her godchild was killed. She lost the security of her family when her parents divorced and her sense of attractiveness when she had to have breast surgery and chemotherapy treatments, which resulted in the temporary loss of her hair. Add to that the loss of her self-esteem from her dismal love relationship that ended in an abortion, and the loss of her good standing at work, and I'd say it was no surprise that Linda became suicidal.

Sound like enough troubles? I think so. And I'd like to be able to say that Linda overcame them. But I'm sorry to say that she hadn't (as of this writing). Although she did not kill herself, at least in the physical sense, she was doing a fine job of committing emotional suicide.

Living with her mother, she locked herself in her room every night upon returning home from work. She would not answer the phone. She had absolutely no life outside of work.

Please don't misunderstand. Linda did have cause to be depressed. She had at least a half dozen reasons for her self-esteem to hit rock bottom. But life goes on! As someone once said, ''After every funeral, no matter how heartbreaking, there comes a time when someone must ask, 'What's for lunch?' ''

Linda was my friend, and she still is my friend, but we no longer enjoy an active friendship. I was there for her for as long as I could afford to be, emotionally speaking. I offered her all the encouragement and support I could give. But she just didn't want to pick herself up. Had I continued to be her ''savior,'' I would have ended up an emotional basket case myself.

DON'T BE A SAVIOR

There's nothing wrong with being a friend to someone who is hurting. That's what friends are for. When my friends are down, I'll do anything I possibly can to be there for them, even if it means canceling plans, rearranging schedules or missing a night of sleep. But I've learned from personal experience that if someone knocked down by life doesn't show interest in getting back up again, then I need to move on as a matter of self-preservation. I just don't have the energy to invest in someone who has no emotional energy at all. I've done it before, and it's a draining, exhausting experience that's detrimental to maintaining high self-esteem. Worst of all, it doesn't help the person who's having a "pity party."

If you allow yourself to become a savior to people riddled with self-pity, you'll not only be frustrated by the experience, but you'll also be crucified the first time they perceive that you've let them down—regardless of the reason. If you haven't discovered this for yourself, trust me. Saviors are supposed to be perfect; when they fall short, they are perceived as weak and usually are told so by the very person they would try to save.

Be a friend. Be a good friend. Be a best friend. Be a "blood sibling," if you must. But don't be a savior. If you do, you might as well build your road leading to the edge of a steep cliff. And when you fall—and you will—it will be nobody's fault but yours.

If you must save someone, save yourself by leaving the "poor little me's" alone.

GETTING BACK UP AGAIN

You know from experience that life can be tough. If you didn't know it, I doubt you'd be reading this book. We all get knocked down from time to time. The only way to avoid it is to involve yourself with no one, and building a road can be awfully lonely if it doesn't intersect with other people's roads.

When life knocks us down, we usually find that our confidence is shaken, which makes it difficult to think and act positively. If we can redirect our negative energy into a positive, success-oriented circumstance, we'll find the way to get back on our feet.

The news of my brother's death in Vietnam knocked

me down hard. For a while, I thought I'd never recover. But, as I mentioned in Chapter Two, realizing that he died while building his road in his chosen direction was an emotionally gratifying experience that helped me to get back up and get on with building my own road.

There's something positive in every negative experience. If nothing else, there is a lesson to be learned. For example, if you experience a setback because you made a mistake or trusted the wrong person, then the lesson here is to learn not to make the same mistake or trust the same person again.

Many times setbacks offer opportunities. Alexander Graham Bell invented a device he hoped would serve as a hearing aid for a deaf relative. Unfortunately for the relative, the device failed to serve that need. But, fortunately for the rest of the world, the device made a fine telephone.

Be positive. Learn to look for the bright side of every disappointment. You can learn some valuable lessons that will help you in the construction of your road.

MAINTAINING CONFIDENCE
AND A POSITIVE ATTITUDE

There are other strategies we can use to maintain our confidence and positive attitude. Let's look at a few.

1 Avoid anger, worry and guilt. These three emotions will quickly erode your self-confidence and positive attitude, because they create self-imposed anxiety and distress. Anger might be a natural emotion, but it's one we choose to feel when people act in ways we don't like.

And it's also a non-productive emotion. If we can take positive, corrective action, then we should. If not, we can choose to put distance between ourselves and the offending parties. Honest guilt is a sign that we need to apologize. Others in our life might try to make us feel guilty for various reasons, but they won't succeed unless we let them. As for worry, it's simply wasted effort. Never has worry accomplished anything positive. We can't affect situations beyond our control, so why worry about them? And if a situation is within our control, it seems more productive to do something constructive instead of wasting energy worrying.

2 Conquer fear through education. Fear also can be detrimental to our self-confidence and positive attitude. Fear is a sign that we need more information before making a decision. If we're afraid of being in the water, perhaps it's because we don't know how to swim. If we're afraid to tackle a project at work, it might be because we don't know enough about it to proceed. When fear throws a road block in your path, education can help you get back to the business of building your road.

3 Act positively and confidently. Do feelings precede actions, or do actions precede feelings? A strong case can be made to support either view. Certainly, we frequently act the way we feel. But professional actors often find themselves feeling the way they act. They cry when they're acting sad, and they involuntarily tremble when they're acting afraid. So when you feel your positive attitude and self-confidence waning, why not try acting positively and confidently? There is a good chance it will produce positive results.

4 Look positive and confident. If acting the part can help, we might as well look the part, too. Project a positive, professional, "real world" appearance. Others judge us by the images we create. Appropriate dress, skillful communication and impressive body language play a large part in making a good first impression, which can help us feel more positive and confident.

Building our own roads requires self-confidence and positive attitudes. It's vital to keep them in top form.

We've talked a lot in this section about what it takes to build your own road. But do you know where your road is going? The decision is entirely up to you. So let's move on to the next section, which deals with building your own road. The next chapter will help you decide its destination.

II

BUILDING YOUR OWN ROAD

5

Destination: Success on Your Own Terms

Successful people are not gifted; they just work hard—then succeed on purpose.
—G. K. NIELSON

It has been said that the world consists of three types of people—those who make things happen, those who watch things happen and those who wonder what happened. In which category do you think most people belong?

I'm not sure whether most people are watchers or wonderers. But I'm pretty certain that the makers are in the minority. Comparatively few people take the initiative to build their roads in chosen directions. Too often, people allow the courses of their roads to be decided by circumstances, fate or even other people.

For example, a person might succumb to parental pressure to enroll in medical school, even though he or she would prefer to be a salesperson. Or an executive might put a career on "auto-pilot" by adopting the corporation's plan for his or her life. These are the people in life who watch what happens and react accordingly. Of course, if we try to build and travel roads designed by other people, we might become bitter and resentful if we don't like the trip, not to mention the destination.

If you're taking an automobile trip and suddenly discover you're on the wrong road, does it make sense to continue driving in that direction? I don't think so, and I'm sure you don't, either. In life, it's not unusual for us to discover sometimes that we've built our roads in the wrong directions. This happens when we find ourselves in the wrong professions, in the wrong marriages, in the wrong company or just plain in the wrong, period.

But what do we do about it? Many times, we simply wonder what happened. Other than that, we sometimes continue to build roads in the wrong direction. We assume—and perhaps correctly—that it's easier to continue building in the wrong direction than it is to change courses. Be that as it might, continuing in the wrong direction is not nearly as rewarding as determining the right route and building our roads in that direction. Nor is it as much fun.

HOW DO WE GET ON THE WRONG ROUTE?

If you think your road is going in the wrong direction, don't feel alone. You've got plenty of company. Studies show that a majority of the employees in the United States would rather be working other jobs, and many of these people actually detest their current jobs. Statistics show that in some states, the divorce rate is about 50%, meaning that one out of two marriages is only temporary.

How do so many roads get going in the wrong direction? Perhaps it's because we often start building roads leading to career and marriage when we're very young, very inexperienced and very naive. In other words, we think we know where we want to go. And, at least for that period of our lives, we probably do.

But life changes as we get older. We become wiser, more experienced and more knowledgeable. We often discover that decisions we made in our youth are no longer satisfactory. The spouse, career, friends and practices we chose might no longer satisfy our needs.

Too many people live with the mistakes they've made in their pasts. They stay locked in the same unsatisfying jobs, marriages, friendships and habits they developed at a time when they might not have had an idea what was best for them. And by the time they realize they're not going in the direction they prefer, they're too intimidated by their circumstances to change.

Don't misunderstand me. I'm not saying that getting rid of habits, jobs, friends and especially spouses is an easy thing to do. It isn't, and I speak from experience on all four counts. But we are under no obligation to continue to build our roads into the Land of Misery because we unintentionally opted in our past to build them through the Land of Mistakes. Compared to an automobile trip, such strategy makes as much sense as spontaneously deciding to vacation at a less appealing destination because you inadvertently took a wrong turn.

CHANGING THE STATUS QUO

When marriages fail, divorce is the appropriate solution. We might be sorry to hear of friends ending their marriages, but we most often understand and offer our emotional support. This is especially true with couples who were married early in their lives. After all, it's not surprising that such important decisions made by people in their teens or early twenties might eventually prove to be mistakes.

So why is our reaction different when a friend or acquaintance abandons an adequate career to pursue one for which he or she is strong in desire, but weak in actual experience? We often think someone must be crazy to close the door on years of experience in a given field. Yet, the person's decision to enter the original field might have been made at the same point in life as many irresponsible marriage decisions—during teens or early twenties. It's almost as if we're saying that people are entitled to be wrong about marriage decisions made early in life, but that our career decisions must be carved into stone.

That's ironic when you consider that most of us will work for 40 or more years of our lives. Even many solid marriages don't last that long. Understand that I'm not undermining the significance of marriage. Instead, I'm emphasizing the importance of enjoying our chosen career. Of course, career isn't everything in life. But at the rate of 40 or more hours per week for 40 or more years, it certainly claims its share.

If your career isn't satisfying, it's up to you to take matters into your own hands. The chance of us being "discovered" or "rescued" from an unsatisfying existence is practically nil. Orchestrating our own career changes is the only solution.

SUCCESS IS WHAT YOU THINK IT IS

What is success? A police officer investigating a crime might say it's making an arrest. The criminal who committed the crime might say it's getting away clean. Of course, one person's success doesn't necessarily have to result in another person's failure. But it is interesting to note that success, like beauty, is in the eye of the beholder.

Let's take the example of a bag lady who lives on city streets because the lifestyle satisfies her. She might be just as happy in her world as the wealthy chief executive officer of a Fortune 500 corporation is in his or her environment. Since we're talking about people with vast personal differences and ideologies, the bag lady's idea of success most likely would be radically different from the CEO's personal definition. She might have a talent for scavenging for food, while the CEO might have a talent for engineering successful stock transactions. So, when the bag lady locates a discarded portion of a ham sandwich, she might be as elated and fulfilled as the CEO who orchestrates an extremely lucrative stock deal.

Who enjoyed the better success? The answer to that question calls for an opinion. And it doesn't matter what you or I think, because we aren't living either life. If the bag lady is satisfied living on the streets and rummaging through dumpsters for sustenance, then she is entitled to pursue her dream just as much as the CEO is entitled to pursue personal fulfillment by strengthening the corporation.

So what's your idea of success? It can be anything you'd like. Anything that gives you a strong purpose to get out of bed in the morning and get moving in a productive direction (and you also get to define "productive") seems like a good idea to me.

SUCCESS IS IN THE LIVING

Whatever definition you give to success, which is the controlling factor for choosing your road's direction, it had better be something you enjoy from beginning to end. The world is filled with idle dreamers who would very much enjoy being broadway stars, for example. But they would have no part of doing what it takes to get there—working temporary jobs, existing on low wages, living out of a suitcase and coping with frequent unemployment. In other words, they would like to reach the destination, but they aren't willing to build the road leading to it.

First, we simply can't become anything that requires dues we're not willing to pay. It's like wanting a college degree without doing the required homework. Honorary degrees excluded, it just won't happen. And, even if it were possible to attain such a success, what would it be worth? The person with the unearned college degree will be no better prepared to take advantage of the opportunities it could bring than the idle dreamer who suddenly lands a part in a multi-million dollar broadway production.

Second, someone who is willing to spend years at an unenjoyable, unfulfilling career existence to achieve a perceived pleasant outcome very likely will have a rude awakening if he or she does reach the desired destination. If building the road is an unenjoyable experience, the thrill of the destination probably won't compensate for the misery. The success won't be meaningful.

The journey to success must be enjoyed as much as its result. No matter your personal definition of success, I'll bet being happy is part of it. As far as our happiness is concerned, we are living now—not in the future. We might hope to be alive in the future, but now is the only time we're alive. And now is the time we should be happy. We shouldn't endure unhappiness on the premise that it will lead to happiness next week, next year or next decade. If it doesn't materialize, we'll just be that much farther along a road we've built in the wrong direction.

If your success destination is located on the other side of the Land of Misery, you'll be a bitter and broken person if you don't reach it. But if it's located on the other side of the Land of Fulfillment, then no matter what happens, you can't lose. Success must be a journey, not a destination.

SUCCESS IS MAKING YOUR OWN RULES

The traditional concept of success has been to get a job, work hard, don't rock the boat and retire in 30 to 40 years with a gold watch and a pension. Of course, many people who subscribed to this concept discovered that they couldn't eat gold watches, and inflation had eroded the value of their pensions to the point that they could barely eat off of them. That's not my idea of an appropriate reward for keeping your nose to the grindstone for three to four decades.

Money doesn't necessarily have to be a reward of success, but there must be a reward of some kind. And when you define your own success, you not only define your own reward, but you can make your own rules, too.

The road to success is self-designed. We don't have to follow someone else's road unless that's what we want to do. Yet, many people resign themselves to follow someone else's road because they've been trained, conditioned and educated to believe that they're incapable of building their own. So they often "lock-step" themselves on someone else's path. They work to attain someone else's idea of success—and someone else's idea of a reward. If and when they finally reach the point of success, they often find it a hollow experience, because they never had the "ownership" of success that comes from building their own roads.

Again, let me stress that we don't have to build our own career roads. Many people have been satisfied to follow other people's roads. But if you want something that you currently don't have, it will be up to you to build the road that will lead to its acquisition or achievement. And when we build our own roads, we set the rules and the rewards, provided that we're willing to pay our dues, or do what is necessary to succeed.

This doesn't mean that you can't continue to work for other people and, of course, follow their rules—so long as they don't restrain you from building your own road, too. For example, your idea of success might be working your full-time job for basic income and subsidizing it with a part-time job that's related to another field. But if your full-time boss decrees that moonlighting is against company policy, then you'll have a decision to make:

find another full-time boss or cease construction on your own road.

If we allow someone else to define our success and determine the course for the roads we build, then we'll eventually reach the destination they choose for us. Personally, I don't want to give anyone else the responsibility for choosing the destination of the road I travel, and I don't think you do, either. Building our own roads is a privilege that every individual should enjoy.

So if something is wrong with your current route, change it. Don't give away the privilege of designing your life road. If you do, you'll very likely live to regret it.

ASSESS YOURSELF

Before setting a course for your road, there are some vital questions to ask yourself. The answers to these questions will help you draw the blueprint for a smooth, straight road leading to your destination.

1 What do you want to become, achieve or attain? Obviously, this would be the first question. If you want to exercise your body back into shape, earn a college degree, merit a promotion at work or purchase a new home, make a note of it. We must have clear mental images of what we want in our minds to be in the best mental and emotional shape to succeed.

2 What education or experience do you need to realize your ambition? Can you learn through self-education, or is enrollment in a formal education program necessary? If you need experience, can it be obtained before, during or after the educational process? Education is fine, but it will never replace experience. Be sure you don't get so bogged down with learning that you don't get around to doing.

3 What are you willing to sacrifice to build this road? Whenever you're trying to become something you aren't, you've got to sacrifice something you already are. When you try to get something you don't have, you've got to give up something you've already got. No matter what road you build, it's going to cost you. You're going to have to give up something, even if it's only some of your free time.

4 Can you live with making this sacrifice, even if you don't reach your destination? In some cases, you will reach your destinations if you sacrifice long enough. For example, the overweight person, the incessant cigarette smoker and the chronic alcoholic will be free of their addictions if they just stay away long enough from excess food, cigarettes and alcohol. But other ambitions are different. If your goal to become CEO of an organization requires you to spend a great deal of time away from your family—something you'd rather not do if given the choice—will you become bitter if someone else is picked for the position instead? If so, then you're probably headed in the wrong direction in the first place, and you might want to choose another.

5 What can happen to prevent you from realizing your ambition? In other words, what can go wrong. Mr. Murphy promises us that "if something can go wrong, it will.'' It's fine, even preferable, to act positively when taking risks. But prepare yourself for the worst by familiarizing yourself with the worst-case scenario and other unpleasant eventualities that might occur. By doing this, you might be able to take actions to prevent some or all of these possibilities from occurring.

Success is a matter of personal definition. Spend time developing a vision or image of your destination. The more detailed it is, the better your chances of building a road that will lead you to it.

Whatever your idea of success, I think you'll find the next chapter interesting. It will help you develop a plan to bring your vision of success to reality.

6

A Vision of Success

The great thing in this world is not so much
where we are but in what direction we
are moving.
—Oliver Wendell Holmes

Have you enjoyed traveling the road you've built thus
far? To a large extent, I'll bet you have. But, if you're
like the average human being, I'll also bet there are
some areas you've long considered exploring but, for
whatever reason, have never begun construction on the
road to lead you there.

Most people I know—including myself—fall into this
category. Their past roads have taken them to various
points of interest, and their journeys have been rewarding. But their roads have only bordered on areas of fulfillment, leaving them with the desire for more.

That's all right, though. Fulfilling these desires is what
the future is for. The future gives us hope and the chance
to build our roads in directions we've only dreamed about
in the past.

Yet, some people act as if they've lost their last chance
to seek satisfaction. They feel their past roads have led
them so far away from their idea of success that it's

impossible to chart courses leading to personal achievement. So they continue to build their roads in the same,
unsatisfying directions.

NO ACCESS, NO EXIT?

Have you ever been seeking directions to your destination, only to be told, "You can't get there from here."
That's ridiculous. You can get anywhere in this world
from where you are now. And the same is true in life.
You can get anywhere you'd like from wherever you are
now by building your road in that direction.

Of course, you have to be realistic. You can drive
from Seattle, Washington to Tallahassee, Florida by
choosing the proper routes. But if you don't have ample
time and access to a dependable vehicle and sufficient
provisions, you probably would choose not to make the
trip. And, if you do make the trip, there is always the
chance that you might never reach Tallahassee. You
could get lost, sidetracked or even killed in an accident.
It's not a pleasant thought, but life is full of risks.

Similarly, you can design your life road to lead you
to the Presidency of the United States. But without ample
time to gain political experience and support, you'll probably never make it. The Supreme Commissioner of Highways, who oversees all life roads, might call your
highway to a halt before you ever reach the Oval Office.
Sad, but true. We can't always get what we want.

However, you can always give your best effort to
getting what you want. If something is worth having,
it's worth the risk and work it takes to get us there. It's
just a matter of whether we are willing to build our roads

in the right directions. And remember, it's not whether we get there that really matters (although that is the general idea, of course). If the trip itself isn't worth your effort, then neither is your destination.

If your current route isn't taking you where you want to go, change it. No matter where you are in life, you can always alter your course. Second only to the Supreme Commissioner, you always have been and always will be in charge of the direction of your road. And if you want to change its course, then why not start construction in a new direction?

DAYDREAM YOUR DREAM ROAD

Before we can set a course, it's vital to know precisely where we want to go. This might seem like elementary information, but it's worth stating.

Do you ever find yourself daydreaming? Too much of it can make you ineffective. But in small doses, daydreaming is a rejuvenating tonic for a tired mind.

Daydream productively by daydreaming about your desired future. It's the first step toward building a road that will get us where we want to go in the least amount of time and under the most pleasant conditions possible. If you were taking the automobile trip from Seattle to Tallahassee, you could chart a course to suit your desires by consulting a current road map.

But there are no maps for roads that haven't been built. So if time is of the essence—and it usually is—and if you want to choose the most appealing route—and we usually do—then it's absolutely essential to make your own map. Since you'll be going to a place that no one has ever been (remember, no two experiences are exactly alike), the only way you can plot a proper course is by dreaming about your destination, or your desired future.

DAYDREAM DAILY

Daydreams are fine and often fun. Use them as mini-vacations from reality, but don't dwell on them. Instead, spend that time thinking about where you really want your road to go. Even if you already have a crystal clear vision of where you want your road to go, I'd strongly recommend that you devote anywhere from five to 15 minutes per day in a dream. Set aside a time when you're least likely to be interrupted and visualize the future you desire.

Let's do it right. Be specific with your dream. Use your imagination. Let's say you'd like to achieve a certain position in your career. Imagine what it would be like to be in that position. Visualize the type of office you'd have and the type of clothes you'd wear. Envision the type of work you'd be doing and the people you would work with. And don't lose sight of the rewards. Imagine yourself enjoying the perks and fringe benefits such a position would offer.

The visualization process is vital. Remember we discussed the workings of the conscious and subconscious minds in Chapter One. When you visualize an experience, you're using the right hemisphere of your brain—the subconscious mind—which is responsible for visualization and imagination. By imagining yourself successful, you're setting a goal in your subconscious mind. This is vitally important to building a road in your chosen direction, because the conscious and the subconscious minds must be in agreement to achieve a desire.

When the two hemispheres are in conflict, the subconscious will easily overpower the conscious mind. That's why we often have trouble when we swear off anything to which we've become accustomed, whether it be sweets, cigarettes or undesired habits. No matter how badly you consciously want to achieve something, your subconscious mind must be properly conditioned for the success you desire, or you'll be virtually destined to fail.

So the first step of visualizing your future is to consciously make the choice. Through daily dreaming, you can instill conscious decisions in your subconscious mind. Then you'll be ready to go to work, because you'll believe in yourself.

DON'T FORGET TO WORK

Some people daydream about being stranded on a desert island with the man or woman of their dreams. They derive a great deal of pleasure from fantasy. But would they really want to be stranded on a desert island indefinitely? Unlike the lifestyle on the old television series, "Gilligan's Island," the existence would grow quite tiresome in time.

Many people live in a dream world. They have a vision of a fulfilling life road destination. But it's a destination they'll never reach because they aren't willing to take action and build in the right direction. People overweight and out-of-shape might yearn to be trim. But if they refuse to exercise and change their eating habits, fat and flabby is the way they'll remain. A young executive might have an eye on the chief executive officer's job. But the executive who isn't willing to put in the overtime to get the proper training and education probably won't rate a promotion, let alone the top spot in the organization.

You can accept the challenge of any situation you can envision, but you must be willing to put in the time and effort to build your road in that direction. If not, then the scenario you envision is nothing more than an idle daydream.

DRAWING THE BLUEPRINT

To start building a road we need a blueprint. We won't achieve or attain our vision of success without a strong plan to take us from conception to reality.

No matter what your vision of success might be, here's a format you can use to convert it into a workable, step-by-step plan.

1 Long-range goal. This is the vision itself, which generally takes 10 years or longer to bring to reality. Perhaps it's achieving a desired career position or accumulating enough money to retire by age 50. It might be founding your own full-time business or building a second home at a resort area. Whatever your definition of success, put it in the form of a long-range goal. This will be the destination on your road.

2 Intermediate goal. These are goals that lead to the achievement of your long-range goals, and they generally take five years or more to achieve. They might include getting sufficient education that would qualify you for your ultimate career position, or putting a certain amount of money into an investment designed to lead to financial security. Or it might include purchasing property designated for your own business or future vacation home. This goal would represent the mid-point of your road.

3 Short-range goals. These are goals to get you started on the road to your destination, and they generally require six months to a year to achieve. They might include getting a job related to your desired field or accumulating enough money to make a start-up investment toward your retirement fund or toward the purchase of property for your own business or vacation home. These goals would represent the first portions of your personal road.

The lengths of time mentioned for the attainment of these goals are more or less arbitrary. There's no law saying that a long-term goal can't take as many as 30 years to achieve, or as little as eight. Likewise, an intermediate goal might take two years, or as many as 10. And a short-term goal could take three months or five years. The time lengths provided were meant as a general guide. Determine the time lengths of your intermediate and short-term goals by applying them in the context of your long-range goal, or the destination of your road.

But, by all means, do apply time-lengths, or deadlines. If you don't, you'll omit a large portion of your incentive to achieve them. A goal without a time limit is a general type of goal that you just might never get around to achieving. People who are frequently saying that they'll get a new job or invest some money are living by general goals without deadlines. And, many times, they discover that someday never comes.

Give deadlines to your goals, and make them as specific as possible. Furthermore, commit them to writing and read them daily. By doing this, you can build a strong image of success in your subconscious mind, which is precisely what is necessary to get you started on the construction of your road.

BUILD ROADS FOR ALL OF YOUR INTERESTS

Success is not one-dimensional. No matter how high you rise in your career or how much money you make, your life will be empty without fulfilling relationships and other interests. Let's take a look at the various life areas where you might consider building roads.

1 Career. Even though I list this area first, I'm not necessarily saying it's most important. But career is one factor that determines our self-worth. We get fulfillment from what we do, and how well we do it. Also, the reality remains that money is important to anyone who pays bills, and our career is one of the few ways we can legally obtain money.

2 Physical. Too little attention to this area can put a sudden, permanent halt to the construction of all of our roads. To build our life roads, we must be alive and in good health. If you want to condition yourself to make a good showing in a marathon, that's your business. But regular exercise, proper diet and moderation of foods and substances that can be harmful in excess is sufficient for developing and maintaining good health.

3 Educational. Much of what we do in life hinges on how much we know about getting something done. The more we know, and the more we know how to use what we know, the more likely we will be able to contribute to ourself and others.

4 Financial. Beyond paying our bills, it's important to have financial goals. If for no other reason, accumulating sufficient retirement capital will help us continue to pay our bills after we're no longer able to earn money. Of course, money can also help us obtain a lot of other goodies that make life interesting. Financial stability allows us the freedom to live life comfortably.

5 Recreational. Building a road can be hard work. Periodic breaks are necessary for rest and recreation. Pleasant diversions are great for personal rejuvenation, so we can be in top form when we get back to the business of building our roads.

6 Charity/Community. Few things are as gratifying as contributing to others less fortunate than you and to the community in which you live. Knowing that you've built your life road to help yourself and others can be not only rewarding, but it can also be personally beneficial. Reaping what you sow is not just a lesson from the Bible; it's a fact of life.

Lives are fulfilling for those who build roads leading to rewards. It's important to determine everything you want in life, then be willing to build your roads in the proper directions.

PAY TRIBUTE TO THE SUPREME COMMISSIONER

Never forget that you are the only human being who can build your own road, and it must be one of your choosing. You can't build a road on a course that some-one else selects. Even if you could, you'd probably be miserable every step of the way, and that's not the way to build a life road.

But also never forget that there's a higher being. The Supreme Commissioner of Highways is always oversee-ing our construction. If we are dedicated to building our roads in our chosen directions, we might find ourselves getting help from unexpected sources at the times that we need help the most.

I don't know how to explain this, but I know that it's true. Let me tell you a story about how I received help at a time in my life when I wondered whether my life road was headed in the wrong direction.

I was going through the trauma of deciding whether to divorce my husband. We married after a storybook romance, and we had accumulated a great many material items during the 15 years we had been together. We both had excellent jobs, which offered us opportunities to take trips to many interesting places, both in this country and abroad. We had the best of everything. However, I would have gladly traded all of it in return for the love and communication that we didn't have.

Enter Dr. Don Beck, Director for the National Values

Center in Denton, Texas. While working for the U.S. Department of Defense, I frequently hired Don as a consultant to work with the organization's supervisors. It just so happened that Don was staging a seminar for our Command at the time I was experiencing this life crisis.

I didn't tell Don, or anyone for that matter, about my troubles. I tried to go on with life as best I could. Obviously, it wasn't good enough, because Don correctly perceived my depression one day when we were having lunch. He confronted me by saying he sensed something was wrong, and he encouraged me to talk about it. Don has a strong background in psychology and sociology. He knew that I had been "bottling up" my problems, and he knew that my trying to handle them by myself could prove to be a mistake that might have far-reaching emotional consequences.

So I talked and cried, and he listened. He never passed judgment on anything I said, whether my remarks were focused on myself or on my husband. Only when I was finished did he finally speak.

"Lois," he said. "From listening to you these past 20 minutes and knowing how much you love life and how much you value who you are, I believe you are committing emotional suicide. You have drunk the hemlock far too long."

So much for the diagnosis. Then he offered the antidote.

"I am going to give you exactly 20 more minutes to make a decision," Don said. "And if you don't, I'm going to kick you right square in the ass."

I was really offended that he had talked to me so

frankly. It was almost more than I could bear, and I started crying again.

"All the tears in the world won't solve this problem," he said. "You've got to make a decision and live with it."

Don had been very helpful in waking up that side of me that realized that I didn't have to please everybody all of the time. In the process of trying to be and do what my husband expected me to be and do, I almost lost myself.

So I made my decision. I left my husband and started building a new road. If I hadn't, I would have been just another person building a life road in the wrong direction.

Again, Don was someone I didn't see every day. We were literally on opposite ends of the country. But I have always believed that the Supreme Commissioner of Highways orchestrated the intersection of our life roads at a time when I needed it most.

If you believe in the Supreme Commissioner of Highways and stand to benefit from His guidance, it's only proper that you give back some of what you're getting. Whether it be in the form of cash donations, volunteer work, or both, personal contributions designed to benefit the spirit that contributes to you are excellent ways to achieve personal satisfaction and fulfillment.

Believe in a supreme being who will look out for your best interests. When building our life roads, we need all the help we can get. Life is full of risks that are necessary to take if we are to make personal progress. When I divorced my husband there were many risks involved I was willing to take. Remember, there is good in every heartbreak. Several years later, I met Michael. We married a year later, and have enjoyed a wonderful, loving and caring relationship. I also have two teen-aged step-children who have given me a valuable perspective on life.

Often in life, we have to take risks to get ahead. But we must be wise about the risks we take. When we lose, we must bear the burden. Turn to the next chapter, where I'll discuss the concept of risks and explain how you can take them to your best advantage.

7

Road Building Is Risky Business

Progress always involves risks. You can't
steal second and keep your foot on first.
—FREDERICK WILCOX

So far in this section, we've talked about the importance
of designing your own road and how to go about making
a blueprint to guide your construction. But before you
get started with your plan, I'd like to caution you to think
long and hard about the design of your road. It should
be the road you want to travel—not one that someone
else would have you travel. And, equally as important,
it shouldn't be a road that you think someone else would
want you to travel. If you allow yourself to follow a road
designed by someone else, you'll be risking your future
happiness. And, to me, that's a foolhardy risk.

Too many people look to the crowd for guidance.
When it comes to what clothes to wear, what cars to
drive and what neighborhoods to call home, they opt for
the choices approved by the majority. After all, there is
safety in numbers. People who fall into this category live
by the philosophy of, "If we do what everyone else does,
we'll be all right."

But if you follow the crowd, the only thing you can

be sure will happen is that you'll end up at the same place as the crowd. Is that where you want to go?

WHAT DOES THE CROWD DO?

Think about what the majority of people do. They make up the "rat race." They snarl, sneer and sound their horns at each other during morning and evening rush-hours. They vacation at crowded resorts. They listen to Top 40 radio stations and watch top-rated television shows and blockbuster motion pictures. To some extent, they also look alike. They wear the same style of clothes—whatever is "in" at the time—and they have their hair styled in the latest fashions.

They forego investments in their future security to enjoy the trappings of success. They mortgage their futures to enjoy the "here and now," joining exclusive country clubs and buying expensive cars, recreational vehicles and prestigious homes that they really can't afford. Many also are in financial trouble. They are paying off numerous loans, and they have several credit cards, all charged to the limit.

Naturally, the crowd that walks the same road is bound to end up at the same destination. They live in poverty or near-poverty during the final years of their lives. Statistics show that only 3% of American people are financially independent upon retirement. The other 97% depend on pensions and social security, which are increasingly devalued by the ravages of inflation.

It's like Robert Frost's poem, *The Road Not Taken*. When we take "the road less traveled by," our destinations will be different from the one at the end of the crowd's road.

Understand that I'm not criticizing anyone for liking fashionable clothes or hairstyles, Top 40 music, top-rated television shows and blockbuster motion pictures. I've been known to enjoy some selections in each category. If you enjoy vacationing at a crowded resort, there's no reason you should stop. And I'm certainly not telling you what kind of car to drive, where to live or what to do with your free time.

All I'm saying is that for you to truly own your road, it must lead you to things you want to do because they bring you pleasure. And anything you might do to keep up with the Joneses might be taking you farther and farther in a direction you don't want to go, because in most cases, following the crowd will lead us only to the Land of Mediocrity.

Life is a series of decisions. Should we marry this person? Should we have children? Should we take this job? Should we start our own businesses? Should we build a house in this neighborhood? Should we invest in the stock market? Should we invest at all? It seems that we spend our entire lives wondering which direction to build our roads. As poet Frost noted, we frequently are sorry that we cannot travel both directions. But we can't be in two places at one time, and we can't live two lives at once.

All of us must choose the directions we want our roads to extend. And, when we do this, we take risks. Will we be happy with our choices, or will we later regret them? Once the decision is made and the risk is taken, only time will tell.

However, unless the risk is taken, we'll never know.

BE PREPARED WHEN YOU REACH FOR THE BRASS RING

Success doesn't come easily. And the greater the success we seek, the greater the risk involved and the greater the consequences—win or lose.

It's like reaching for the brass ring while riding a carrousel, or a merry-go-round. The farther the reach that's necessary to grab it, the greater the prize. But the farther the rider must stretch to grasp the ring, the greater the chances that he or she will fall.

If you want to travel the well-worn road that's favored by the crowd, you'll play it safe. You won't take necessary chances and risks. You won't take any great falls, but you won't win any great prizes, either.

To gain anything significant, you must take some kind of risk. If you want to be safe with your money, do like the crowd. Deposit your money in the safest interest-bearing vehicle that exists—a passbook savings account. Deposits of up to $100,000 are guaranteed by the Federal Depositors' Insurance Commission (FDIC). This means that we're more or less assured that our money on deposit will be available when we need it.

But let's look at what happens to money deposited in a savings account. Let's say you deposit $1,000 in an account that pays 6% interest. At the end of the year, you'll have $1,060—a net gain of $60. Of course, this $60 is subject to federal and state taxes. And the spending power of what remains in the account is subject to inflation, which at best generally runs about 5% and has been known to be as high as 18% during the early 1980s. In other words, at the end of one year, the spending power of the after-tax money in your account might be at best equal to—but more likely less than—what it was when it was deposited.

Sure, a savings account is safe. But it should be, if you're losing spending power to keep it there.

On the other hand, you can invest your money in oil drilling or motion pictures. The rate of return is extremely high—if the investments pay off. But the success rate of these ventures is extremely small. Chances are good that you'll lose your investment altogether. But that's the risk you take if you would seek significant rewards.

IF YOU WOULD GAIN ANYTHING, YOU MUST RISK SOMETHING

Whatever we might seek to gain in life, it's necessary to risk something. I can't think of a single exception. If we seek to gain relationships, whether they involve potential friends or mates, we run the risk of rejection. If we take on new jobs, we must forfeit our old ones and run the risk of not surviving our probationary periods. If we form our own businesses, we risk the money we invest and any collateral we put on the line to obtain start-up capital. When we put ourselves into long-term debt to purchase a car or a home, we run the risk of losing the item should future circumstances prevent us from paying the mortgage. Even if we seek to develop relationships with wealthy people who would support us in grand style for the rest of our lives, we run the risk of losing our self-respect and self-esteem.

There is no way around risk—except not to take it. But then, we won't have friends or mates. We'll stay at our first jobs, and we'll never own anything significant. And without risk, we'll never be anything significant, either, because all physical, mental and emotional growth involves some degree of risk.

Of course, we shouldn't take risks for the sake of taking risks. It's one thing to risk your life to rescue your child from a burning building; it's quite another thing to risk your life for the thrill of balancing on one foot upon the seat of a motorcycle traveling 65 miles per hour. (Believe me, I've heard of people doing this.)

Great risks must be reserved for great gains. A person who is willing to take great risks for small gains probably will never reach the intended destination. He or she either will be emotionally devastated, financially ruined or actually killed, because the odds of meeting with undesired results increase with the number of risks we take.

It's like passing a car on a two-lane highway. Sensible people don't even attempt it unless they are absolutely certain they can pull out into the next lane, complete the pass and return to their own side of the road with time to spare before meeting an oncoming vehicle. Yet, I'm sure you've seen your share of motorists who are anything but sensible. They subject themselves—and innocent oncoming motorists—to great risk to gain a mere position in a long string of traffic. And I'm sure you've also had occasion to see the wreckage of motorists who took great risks and lost.

People who take great risks for insignificant gains are

fools who deserve to lose. But people who take great
risks for great gains understand that there is a price to
pay for everything. They are the ones who carefully
weigh what they risk against what they stand to gain. If
the risk is worth it, then they go for it. And, because
they know their desired reward is worth the risk, they
are better prepared to accept the outcome, be it success
or failure.

When we're motivated by inspiring goals, we should
be willing to take the risks, enjoy the journey and enjoy
the consequences—win or lose. As they say, "It is better
to have loved and lost." Much better. Likewise, it is
better to have risked for something great and lost, than
never to have risked for something great at all. Even our
losses offer us something valuable. If nothing else, they
offer us the chance to make a fresh start—this time with
greater knowledge that comes from experience.

MAKE YOUR OWN CHOICES

I can't even pretend to be able to orchestrate your best
possible life. Only you can do that. But I can offer you
a general guideline to follow: always try to be in a position where you have attractive options.

The most frustrating times in our lives occur when we
are faced with unpleasant situations for which we have
no desirable alternatives. For example, our job descrip-
tion is redefined, leaving us holding the short end of the
stick. But we can't afford to quit because we don't have
any new job prospects, and we don't have sufficient
resources to allow us to survive a period of voluntary
unemployment. We have a golden opportunity to travel

abroad inexpensively with friends, but we must turn down the opportunity because we can't afford taking several weeks off from work. A child needs braces that we can't afford because we're financially strapped paying our current bills.

No matter what you do, there will be times when you won't have attractive choices. Life will throw you a situation, and you'll have to make the best of it. For example, your doctor might tell you that modern medical science is powerless to prevent you from going blind. In such a situation, you'd just have to learn to cope. But the fact remains that the best lives belong to people who are in a position to make choices. And as a rule, there is one thing that separates people who have attractive alternatives and those who don't.

Money.

It isn't everything in life, but it does provide the ability to make choices. With sufficient money, we can turn down jobs we don't want and quit jobs we don't want to keep. With money, we can take time off from work when we want, and we can go where we want during our vacations. Even in our day-to-day lives, money allows us plenty of options when it comes to choosing the food we eat, the clothes we wear and the neighborhood in which we reside.

Of course, personal satisfaction and career fulfillment play a large role in career choices, and these ideals should not be overlooked when determining the course of your road. After all, money can't buy you intrinsic rewards; only making a career and life of doing what you enjoy can bring you fulfillment.

Whatever direction you choose for the road you build,

the ultimate choice you can make is to be a success. And the ultimate success you can attain will be the lifestyle that allows you the privilege of choice.

Almost always, we have to take risks to get there.

QUESTIONS TO ASK
WHEN CONTEMPLATING RISKS

Risks might be unavoidable if you would make progress, but that's no reason in itself to throw caution to the wind. Remember, intelligent risks must be measured against what we stand to gain.

The fact that many states have lotteries proves that many people wouldn't hesitate to risk $10 for a chance, however slim, at winning a million dollars or more. But if the price of lottery tickets were a hundred times as much, who would buy them? Few people would be willing to risk $1,000 on a remote chance of becoming millionaires.

So whenever we consider risking anything—whether its money, time, effort or emotions—it's vital that we ask ourselves some questions. Here are a list of questions to consider before taking any kind of risk. The answers they yield will help you review your personal situation so you can make the most intelligent decision.

1 Why must the status quo be changed? Is there a real desire or need for change? That is, will the desired change significantly increase the quality of your life? Is the status quo really inconducive to achieving your definition of happiness and fulfillment? Or are you seeking the change to impress others?

Be careful about taking any risk designed primarily to gain the attention of others. First, if the risk fails, you might get others' attention, but it might not be the kind you would want. For example, if an unsuccessful financial risk forces you into personal bankruptcy, you'll be the talk of your neighborhood. But who wants that kind of attention? Furthermore, if your risk proves successful, you might be disillusioned to discover that the very people you most wanted to impress possibly couldn't care less about your success. (And those who did care might malign you, anyway.)

The first law of intelligent risking states that any risk (short of saving a loved one's life) that requires your life, liberty or happiness as collateral simply isn't worth it. What can you possibly gain that's worth more? I'm not saying we can't appreciate attention from others when we succeed. For example, a person who has made the long trek from obesity to physical fitness might very much enjoy hearing others' compliments. But the impetus for getting into shape most likely was to develop good health, and high self-esteem. In other words, the individual weathered the hardships first and foremost for himself or herself. That's all that really matters.

If the change in status quo you seek is absolutely necessary to ensure your continued happiness—not continued complacency—then you've passed the first test.

2 Is the risk necessary? Is there another way the same end can be achieved without taking a risk? If so, pursue that course of action. Like pain and suffering, unnecessary risk should be avoided if at all possible. For example, why give up a career position you enjoy to start your own business if you don't foresee any significant financial or intrinsic gain? Only when risk is absolutely necessary to achieve your desired goal should it even be considered at all. Why take a gamble, however small, at losing something valuable if it's not necessary to lose it at all?

3 Can the risk be minimized? In some cases, it probably can. When dealing with financial investments, the greater the rate of return, the greater the odds of losing your capital. If it's vital for you to raise a significant sum of money within a relatively short period of time, it might be necessary to choose a high-risk investment. But if you're 35 years old and are investing for your retirement, there's no rush. You can minimize your risk by choosing a lower-yield but relatively safer investment.

4 Who else will be hurt by a risk that fails? It's one thing for us to take the punishment for our failures. But if innocent people must suffer, is the risk worth it? If you're single, it might be worth it to you to put your home on the line for a business venture, knowing that you can adjust to life in an efficiency apartment if the risk fails. But if you're married with four children, an Irish setter and a German shepherd, it might not be fair to subject them to such a penalty.

5 What will happen if we lose? Take some time to think about this one. Visualize in your mind the worst-case scenario and imagine yourself coping with it. When we take risks to change the status quo, we automatically lose the status quo, for better or worse. And if we can't handle the worst, then we'd better not take the risk.

Remember, there is no interesting life without risk. But if the risk isn't carefully considered, your life might be worse than it would have been had you taken no risk at all. Be cautious with the risks you take when building your road. Ill-considered risks can make future construction very tough.

I hate to close this chapter with bad news, but let's face reality. Sometimes, even our most carefully considered risks will fail. It's not a comfortable thought, but that's life. No one likes to fail, but even failing isn't all bad. I'll tell you more about why this is so in the next chapter.

8

Failure Is Only a Pothole, Not a Pit

Constant effort and frequent mistakes
are the stepping-stones of genius.
—ELBERT HUBBARD

Let me share a secret with you: Failure doesn't really exist, unless you give life to it.

I closed a previous chapter by telling you the story of my divorce. We were married for 15 years. Everything started out great, and it continued that way for several years.

I'll skip the gory details and get right to the point. In the minds of many, my marriage failed. But did it? Did I fail? Absolutely not. I could have chosen to fail, if that's what suited me. I chose not to see it as a failure.

Whether we fail or not is a matter of opinion. Had I chosen to view my 15-year marriage as a failure, I probably would recall it with bitterness. After all, the Supreme Commissioner of Highways allots us about 70 or so years here on earth (figures are subject to fluctuation, depending on fate and personal lifestyle). And 15 years is almost one-fourth of that allotment. Had I chosen to fail, I probably would view that period in retrospect as a terrible waste of some of the best years of my life.

I didn't fail, because I chose to learn instead.

FAILURE IS JUST ANOTHER WORD
FOR LEARNING

I don't look at my first marriage as a failure; instead, I look at it as a learning experience.

I learned many lessons during my first marriage. I believe my second marriage has benefited immensely from the lessons I learned in my first. I now recognize that my first marriage was simply part of the road I built that led to my current marriage.

Many times, society attaches the failure label after superficially viewing a person's circumstances. When a business folds, we call it a failure. Yet, R. H. Macy "failed" in business seven times before opening the world-famous Macy's Department Store in New York City. When a baseball player sets a record for strike-outs, we might view him as a failure. Yet, the legendary Babe Ruth did just that. He also set a record for hitting home-runs that stood for several decades. As a young man, Walt Disney initially failed as a cartoonist. Yet, more than 20 years after his death, his name and the names of his most popular creations—Mickey Mouse, Donald Duck and associates—remain household words. By using society's standards, Abraham Lincoln failed many times as a businessman and as a politician. The fact that his face is carved on Mount Rushmore near Rapid City, SD, indicates that he is regarded as one of the greatest U.S. presidents in history.

So let's face it. Failure or perceived failure might not

feel good, but it's really not so bad. When we view it as a learning experience, it's actually the route to success. So-called failures usually result from mistakes, or a series of mistakes. And what is a mistake? A mistake is a decision we make with the information, perceptions and knowledge we hold at the moment we take the action. But after learning from our mistakes, we develop new information, perceptions and knowledge that we can use to make new and hopefully better decisions.

There are only two times when "failure" is really a failure. We truly fail when we:

1 Don't learn from our mistakes. If we act in ways to produce unfavorable results, the lesson is to not act the same way again. As simple as this might look on paper, it's a lesson that some people are slow to learn. Sometimes, they deny having made mistakes at all. So they continue to repeat their mistakes—and suffer the same unfavorable consequences. At this point, the first experience becomes a failure, because it produces absolutely nothing positive.

2 Quit. Failures offer invaluable lessons that can help us succeed. But if we stop trying to succeed, we stop building our roads in our preferred direction. Lessons can help us only when we're willing to apply what we've learned to our future. If we're not willing to carry on, the lessons we learn are wasted, and the experience can be classified as a failure.

Mistakes (actions that others may call failures) are stepping stones to success, only if we have learned from the experience and are willing to continue building our roads. Otherwise, they can rightfully be classified as failures.

THE FEAR OF FAILURE

In this world, there are many winners. These are people who are accustomed to winning, and they expect to win when they undertake new endeavors. There also are losers. These are people so accustomed to losing that they don't even consider undertaking new ventures, and if they do, they know they will lose. The difference between the two often amounts to the fear of failure. Most of us have it at some point in our lives. Winners overcome it. Losers do not.

We were more or less conditioned to fear failure as children. In school, we were penalized for being wrong. If we missed answers on tests, our grades reflected our errors. If we offered the wrong answer during a class discussion, we had to suffer the embarrassment of being wrong in the presence of our peers. I have always wondered whether that ever happened to Abraham Lincoln, who is credited with saying, "It is better to remain silent and be thought a fool than to open your mouth and remove all doubt."

Peer pressure is a particularly intense factor in building the fear of failure. Few of us were good at everything as children. (Few of us still are as adults.) When we displayed our below-average skills in athletics, academics or the arts, we usually were rewarded with ridicule and, sometimes, scorn. For example:

"You're such a lousy softball player. You lost the game for us."

"You're so dumb! You don't know anything."

"You call that art?"

"You might call that singing, but I call it hog-calling."

Children can be awfully cruel, and so can many adults. Such callous remarks can hurt a child's self-esteem, causing him or her to plummet into despair. When that happens, it's not unusual for the child to avoid the difficult activity and seek no further development. From the child's standpoint, it's easier on his or her self-esteem to cease development than it is to be ridiculed.

That might be all right for children. But by the time we're adults, we'd better determine what is most important to us. We have a choice—building roads in our chosen directions or letting our courses be dictated by our fears of what others might think of us.

People who attach less significance to their personal development than to the opinions of their peers often choose to spare themselves the misery of embarrassment. They see themselves as losers. If they do make a vain attempt to succeed, their perceived failure merely reinforces their losing attitude and lowers self-esteem. As a result, these people are losers who deserve to lose, not because they are second-class people, but because losing is what they do best.

When we fear failure, we also fear success. There is no way we can succeed at anything without running the risk of failure. If you would succeed at any endeavor, you must run the risk of failing or learning.

FEAR OF FAILURE IS A ROADBLOCK

The fear of failure is a barrier we must overcome if we're to succeed at anything. I can think of no better story to illustrate this point than the movie L. Frank Baum's *The Wizard Of Oz*.

After a tornado whisked her away from Kansas, Dorothy suddenly found herself in the Land of Oz, where she befriended a brainless scarecrow, a heartless tin man and a cowardly lion. Together, they sought the wizard, whom they believed could grant their wishes by giving them what they lacked.

The Wizard of Oz didn't grant idle wishes. Before he would grant their requests, the wizard demanded something as an offering of good faith—the broomstick belonging to the Wicked Witch of the West.

Of course, the mere prospect of success in that venture struck fear into their hearts (except for the Tin Man, who didn't have one, but was afraid just the same). They feared the result of failure, which very likely would have meant their deaths. (Sometimes in life, the fear of failing to achieve our goals can be worse than the fear of death.)

But they set off in pursuit of their goal. They knew what they wanted, and they were willing to risk all to get it. Overcoming a host of obstacles, they found themselves inside the witch's castle. The final obstacle they overcame was their fear of the witch, who eventually cornered and prepared to kill them. When the wicked witch set fire to the scarecrow, Dorothy forgot her fear and extinguished the blaze with water, which splashed onto the wicked witch's face, dissolving her Royal Wickedness. (Isn't it true in life that when we act in the face of fear, the fear dissolves?)

Successful, the four returned to the wizard for the brain, heart, courage and home he had promised them. But they found that the great wizard was only a meek, mild-mannered man hiding behind an intimidating facade operated by powerful machinery.

The wizard had been exposed! He didn't have a brain for the scarecrow, a heart for the tin man or courage for the lion. Yet, all three had proven themselves worthy of their requests during their quest for the witch's broomstick. After the witch captured Dorothy, the scarecrow devised a plan to rescue her. That required planning and common sense, or "brains." When the scarecrow had been torn apart by the witch's army, the tin man helped put him back together again. He also offered encouragement and support when the hesitant lion badly needed it. That required compassion, or "heart." Even the "cowardly" lion allowed his friends to cling to his tail as they climbed the mountain leading to the witch's castle. That required fortitude and determination, or "courage."

So the wizard merely confirmed these qualities in each character. He gave the scarecrow a diploma, something that many people without "brains" have managed to achieve. He gave the tin man a clock that ticked like a heartbeat. Even callous, heartless people have pulses. And he gave the lion a medal of valor, something that many people have earned for performing so-called courageous acts while frightened out of their wits!

With these gifts, each of the three became fulfilled. The irony is that all three of them already possessed the potential to achieve personal fulfillment. They merely needed someone to confirm it. In real life, we often allow our potential to lie dormant because we're waiting for someone to "knight" us as being grown up, intelligent, compassionate and courageous. And like these storybook characters, we, too, have all the potential we need to achieve fulfillment.

Too often in life, we're like the scarecrow, tin man and cowardly lion. We seek confirmation from "exalted" figures—people like the wizard. These exalted people develop power by building their own self-esteem at the expense of other people's self-esteem. When we devote our energies to gaining their favor, we often find ourselves involved in physically, mentally and emotionally (and sometimes financially) expensive and exhausting endeavors that ultimately prove frustrating. No one can grant us the power to become anything that we can't become by ourselves. Expecting otherwise is a waste of time, energy and potential that could be applied to building your road to success.

Furthermore, no one can be "exalted" unless you give them that power. So rather than exalt, why not ignore people who would criticize or belittle your abilities and ambitions. The wizard gained power and strength by the fact that people revered him. Had they ignored him, he would have been just another eccentric madman who lived in a castle.

As for Dorothy, the wizard couldn't help her, either. She had to realize that no one can help anyone achieve fulfillment. It's an inside job. Happiness and fulfillment don't lie in another state of the union. Happiness and fulfillment is a state of mind. When she realized that, Dorothy could go home again and continue building her own road.

No one can intimidate you unless you allow it. Believe in yourself, and your ability to succeed. Sure, you'll probably "fail" occasionally along the way. But as long as you learn from the experience, you'll keep growing and building better roads.

IF LOSERS DESERVE TO LOSE, WHAT DO WINNERS DESERVE?

Prior to my retelling of *The Wizard of Oz*, I pointed out that losers deserve to lose because they see themselves as losers and are too afraid to make an effort to change that perception.

So what do winners deserve? They deserve to win. They see themselves as winners. They don't let fear of failure and possible ridicule prevent them from building their road to success. And when they make mistakes, winners don't view them as failures. Instead, they learn from them, and apply the new information to future endeavors.

For example, the majority of Apollo ships were off-course at some time during their flights to and from the moon. Of course, allowing them to remain off-course would have spelled doom for the crew, because the ships would have missed their destinations and traveled on into infinity. Yet, that's exactly what would have happened had members of the crew and the National Aeronautics and Space Administration's Houston Control Center become discouraged and given up upon realizing that the voyages weren't going precisely as planned.

Of course, the American people—not to mention the crew—would have found such an attitude totally unacceptable. And so would NASA. So when it was discovered that the spaceship was off-course, the crew and the control center worked together to get it back on course. This process was repeated numerous times—as many times as was necessary to put the ship on the moon and to bring it back to earth safely.

Winners operate the same way. They don't become emotionally paralyzed when reality doesn't coincide precisely with their visions. They don't put the construction of their roads indefinitely "on hold" to analyze and agonize over what went wrong. They carefully set courses for their roads and begin construction. And, like the Apollo crew and support staff, when they discover their roads are off-course, they immediately concentrate efforts on getting them back according to plan. Certainly, winners prefer to build straight roads leading to their destinations. But they realize that external circumstances and personal errors might cause their roads to go astray, resulting in occasional bends and turns necessary to put them back on course.

Winners are committed to reaching their destinations. They are willing to persevere. In their efforts to succeed, they are willing to make more mistakes, because they know mistakes will result in more knowledge that will increase their chances of success. And they are willing to make mistakes until they succeed.

That's the price of success. There is nothing special about people who win. They're just willing to pay the price. And people who are willing to pay the price to win deserve to win.

"FAILURES" CAN LEAD US IN NEW DIRECTIONS

Sometimes, mistakes or unforeseen circumstances can knock our roads so far off-course that it might be easier and more productive to change our destinations. For example, the CEO of an electric typewriter manufacturing company that went bankrupt upon the introduction of word processors and computers might devote attention to another endeavor, rather than try to revive the old corporation.

Let me give you an actual example of someone who changed his destination when his original plans went awry. In 1960, Bill Alley set a world record after hurling a javelin 283 feet and eight inches. Unfortunately, an irreversible ailment to his right arm ended his career as an athlete.

But armed with an engineering degree, Alley set out to manufacture aluminum-shafted javelins, which had better aerodynamics than the wooden variety. There wasn't a huge market for javelins. But Alley noticed that a javelin's handle resembled the shaft of a golf club. With golf being a popular sport, Alley decided to go into the business of manufacturing golf putters.

Unfortunately, he designed the formula incorrectly. When a weight was attached to one of the putters fresh off the assembly line, the club bent a whopping 17 inches—folding almost in half—instead of the normal two-inch bend.

In frustration, Alley bent one of the putters over his knee. Then he was struck with a capital idea. Rather than try to correct the problem, why not create an opportunity. He immediately purchased space in a magazine advertising the clubs as "Silly Putters"—a novelty for the temperamental golfer. He priced them at $19.95 each and received orders for 6,000.

With the income he received, Alley was able to pursue new opportunities. To make a long story short, his company is called the REC Corporation of Stowe, VT, and he employs up to 35 people and generates up to $2 million annually in revenues. The company manufactures items from carbon fiber, including blood pumps for dialysis machines, cross-country ski poles, violin bows, phonograph arms, artificial limbs and automotive drive shafts— all this from someone who "failed" to make a decent golf club.

Mistakes and failures aren't all bad. As Bill Alley discovered, they sometimes can be blessings. At worst, they are teachers, and we should view them as such.

There are other teachers from whom we can learn valuable lessons about success. They are called mentors, and the next chapter will discuss the significance of having strong mentors in our lives to help us build our roads in the right directions.

9

Role Models Show the Way

Example is not the main thing in influencing others. It is the only thing.
—ALBERT SCHWEITZER

Do you have a mentor? If not, find one. Better yet, find several. There is nothing that can help you build better, straighter roads toward success, fulfillment and the enjoyment of life itself more than loving, caring guidance from people who have already made a lot more progress on their roads than you have on yours.

Mentors are significant, special people in our lives. They help us develop by teaching us, encouraging us to succeed and reassuring us when we're discouraged. They entertain and inform us with stories about themselves and their experiences. They guide us by sharing their beliefs, and the success they enjoy offers a positive and inspiring example of what we can become and aspire to.

Most importantly, mentors help us feel good about ourselves. In this first chapter, we discussed the significance of the comments we hear from people we respect and the impact these remarks deliver to our self-esteem. Mentors are positive people who speak to us in positive terms. With life's way of tearing us down all too frequently, it's refreshing to be rebuilt through a rewarding relationship with someone who cares enough to influence us positively.

MEET MY FIRST MENTOR

One of the most powerful influences in my life has been my father, Larry Lyden. He has been a mentor to me all of my life in many ways. He's approaching 80 years of age, but you would never know it to look at him. He's a lively gentleman who is constantly whistling. He has never lost the bounce in his step and the "snap" in his personality.

He's very firm in his beliefs. He's not without his weaknesses. He is an alcoholic. He has great strengths, and he has been sober for more than a dozen years. But regardless of his state of sobriety, he has always been one of the most caring and loving people I have ever known. There has been a strong bond between us for as long as I can remember. Although I was one of eight children, Dad always had a way of making me feel special. I can remember him cuddling me as a child, making me laugh when I was sad and, above all, treating me like I was special and not just another mouth that needed to be fed.

Dad instilled in me some powerful life insights. He has never done anything "by the book." He has built his own road his own way, and he has enjoyed his successes. He's not a wealthy man. In fact, Dad and Mom live off social security and the income generated from a lawnmower repair business he operates out of his garage. Yet, he is wealthy in many ways. He's never lost his determination to enjoy life. And each time something positive has happened in my life, Dad has been on hand to cheer me on, always reminding me how proud he is of me.

I have always taken my problems to Dad. He has always told me, "Lois, I can't solve your problems, but you can talk with me about them." Many times, I have found that talking out my problems revealed a solution. Dad always looks on the good side of every situation, and he taught me how to do that early in life. Just that ability alone has helped me weather a lot of stormy situations.

Dad isn't well educated in the academic sense. In fact, he jokes that he was kicked out of the third grade because he wouldn't shave. Yet, he has taught me things I never learned in school, or even college, for that matter. For starters, he taught me that love of self and other people is essential to getting through life with any semblance of sanity. And watching him live his beliefs has shown me that loving others is a lot more fun—and productive— than living a life full of hate, bitterness and resentment.

DAD TAUGHT ME ABOUT BUILDING ROADS

Most importantly, Dad was the person who taught me the importance of building my road into the future. I learned this at the tender age of four, when I worked my first "job" as a milkman. Actually, Dad was the milkman—the best milkman in the territory. That's what he told me, and that's what I believed.

I don't remember the exact day I began working the milk route with Dad, but I do remember some of the adventures we had. I wore bib overalls—just like Dad's, except mine were made of corduroy. They were our uniforms. Dad started his route at 4:30 A.M. Three hours later, he'd swing by our house and pick me up. Every night when I went to bed, I looked forward to the next morning with eager anticipation, because I loved riding on the milk truck, and I simply adored my dad.

Since I was very tiny in stature, Dad built for me a seat out of two milk crates and positioned it on the passenger side of the truck. He tied a rope through the handles so I wouldn't tumble about. But best of all was that he made the seat high enough for me to see outside. We made our daily rounds singing songs, learning words from signs and billboards, talking to customers and laughing. We were very good at laughing. At times, the roads were rough. Michigan winters are known for their destruction of paved streets. Some of the roads annoyed me because they caused the milk bottles to clink and my teeth to gnash.

One day, I asked Dad, "Why doesn't somebody fix this road?"

"I don't know," he said. "Sometimes, we have to travel rough roads. If it's important enough for you to get where you're going, then you won't mind traveling a rough road and making the best of it." Then he'd say something to make me laugh, and I'd forget about all the bumps and the jolts.

On another day, Dad decided that one of the roads was simply too rough for the truck to handle, so he detoured on another road that we didn't usually take.

"No, no!" I yelled. "Daddy, we've got to go to the next road!"

Dad just smiled. "Sometimes, if a road is too rough to ride, we simply have to take another road."

Of course, I didn't immediately perceive the significance of these lessons. But as I got older, I understood how they applied to our lives. Sometimes, the roads leading to our destinations are rough. We can either choose to forget about going where we want, or we can do our best to cope with the rough road. And if our vision of self-defined success is important enough for us to achieve, we won't mind taking the rough roads.

But sometimes if a road is simply too rough for travel, we can find an alternate route. For example, I would have preferred going to college for four years immediately after graduation from high school. Lack of money ruled out that option. But Dad always told me, "If you can't get what you want one way, find another way to get it." I found another road. It was a long one, and even that road was rough at times. It took me 22 years of night school to earn my bachelor's degree in business administration. But I finally got it because I was willing to take the road leading to it.

I could go on forever about the lessons I've learned from Dad. But one of the most recent lessons that has helped guide me as a speaker and trainer involves his work as a lawnmower repairman.

Dad bought a broken-down lawn mower from his neighbor for $10. The mower was in such poor shape that the neighbor felt lucky to get $10 for it. Dad immediately went to work on the machine. He invested a lot of time and effort into restoring it to practically mint condition. Then he sold the lawn mower for $180—to the neighbor who had sold it to him for $10.

At first, the neighbor didn't recognize the mower. He was so impressed with the way it appeared and the sound of its engine that it never crossed his mind it could be the same machine. Dad made sure that his neighbor knew he was buying back his original lawn mower. But the neighbor didn't mind paying 18 times as much as he'd received for it to buy it back, because he felt Dad's effort had made it worth that amount.

The same principle works with human beings. No matter what you think you're worth, you can increase your actual value to yourself and others—if you're willing to put in the time and effort.

KEEP ON MOVING

Another mentor was a woman named Halina Brynski. I met her in July 1966 at the age of 18, when I started to work for the Department of Defense as a clerk.

Halina is a fascinating woman who challenged me early in life. A clerk was the lowest rank of all employees, and I was the lowest salary clerk.

"You're not going to be a clerk forever," Halina told me shortly after I arrived there. "You're very bright, very professional, and you've got to remember always to move on. If you don't keep moving forward or sideways, you turn stale, and you'll grow to be a crotchety old woman." She was echoing the teachings of my father—we should always continue to build our life roads into the future.

Halina also taught me that if we don't enjoy the time and effort involved in the pursuit of our goals, we're defeating our purpose. It's not uncommon to see people pursue their goals with such fervor that they forget to enjoy the daily living. Halina showed me how to be a possibility thinker—to look outside the norm.

Halina was a true mentor, teaching me many things about work and life in general. She truly prepared me well. Fifteen years after our first meeting, Halina retired, and I was selected as her replacement.

DON'T BE TOUGH ALL OF THE TIME

Sometimes, mentors can be our contemporaries who have had greater or different experiences than we have had. Jackie Reid is a colleague who lives in Pendleton, SC. We've conducted many seminars together in a team-teaching form. Jackie has a very soft, quiet approach to life—and she maintains a realistic approach to herself, to life and to the world in general.

The most important thing I have learned from Jackie is that it isn't necessary to be "tough" to get what you want. You don't have to be manipulative, and you certainly don't have to step on anybody's face to climb to the "top of the heap."

Jackie has also helped me recognize that it's all right to do nothing some of the time. Doing nothing is one of the most difficult activities I have ever encountered. To do nothing takes practice. You sit or lay down. Clear your mind of all activity for as long as possible. Success is measured in being refreshed. One minute of doing nothing equates to many hours of activity which follows. Tough people are always moving, thinking and doing just to stay ahead of the "tough game."

I feel sorry for tough people. Most of the time, they're

busy playing the same old game: when meeting people, they quickly find reasons to put them down, criticize or compare. Their self-esteem is so low that they are virtually certain that people who get to know them won't like them. So they beat others to the punch by throwing the first jibe or insult. Not only does such a philosophy prevent them from having true friends, but it also requires a great deal of energy to produce a negative result. I don't mind admitting that I'm too lazy for that kind of work.

People need balance. Sure, times can be tough, and some circumstances can require us to take tough stances. But we need periods when we can drop the tough facade and enjoy peace and harmony. We don't have to be tough all the time.

I learned a similar lesson about being tough from a man. In a civilization where ''real men'' are rough and tough, it was refreshing to meet an exception to the rule. I met General Oscar Decker when I worked for the Department of Defense. From him, I learned that you could be soft and demanding and still have your act together. General Decker proved that by his rank and position as Commander, U. S. Army Take-Automotive Command. He had been tough enough to serve in many confrontations across the globe; yet, he was one of the kindest men I've ever known. He always had time to spend with people who worked with him. No matter how trite or serious an employee's problem or concern was, he always invested the time to sit, listen, advise and discuss. I was a secretary when I first met him, yet he never treated me like an underling. General Decker valued people for who they were and not necessarily for what they could do for him and his career. I admired that quality in him a great deal. He was a gentle man and a genuine gentleman. He had a tremendous influence on me.

DEVELOP MENTORS IN PASSING

Sometimes, we don't have to have a formal relationship with a mentor who makes a significant impact in our lives. In 1975, I attended a seminar staged by speaker Dru Scott. This was during the "blue suit" period of my life, when I believed there were certain "rules" for success.

I was surprised to see Dru approach the podium in a print blouse, short black skirt, black stockings and a long purple scarf. I remember thinking, "Who in the hell is that?"

Then she introduced herself. "My name is Dru," she said. "My father wanted a boy, so he picked out the boy's name in advance. He didn't get a boy, but he liked the name, and that's why my name is Dru."

Then she called attention to her attire.

"Some of you might not like the way I'm dressed, but I'm here to tell you I like dressing this way. I'm not interested in going along with the crowd. I don't have to blend in with the community to be successful. And neither do you. Don't be like everybody else. Find yourself first, and then the world will find you."

It's going on 15 years since I attended that seminar, but I still remember Dru's words. And I'm sure I always will.

MENTORS CAN BE COACHES

Mentors sometimes serve as coaches in life. One of my mentors was really a coach. Dorothy Demrick taught physical education at my old high school. She was an interesting lady in many respects, but the most impressive quality about her was that she truly cared about teens— and about me.

Dottie, as she was lovingly known by her fellow teachers, taught gym class, which included a six-week segment on gymnastics. One day she approached me after class.

"You know, you're really very good on the balance beam," she said. "I'd like to work more with you, if you'd like."

Working together, we determined that my strength in gymnastics lay in balancing. The balance beam was a four-inch wooden bar situated about four to five feet off the ground. Few young ladies were interested in this sport in my day, because they were afraid of falling. I had always been interested in ballet and modern dance, and with Dottie's encouragement, I worked up the enthusiasm to tackle the beam. I viewed it as dancing on a four-inch piece of wood.

I would work out for two hours every day after school. After months of practice, Dottie approached me and said the magic words:

"I think you're ready for competition."

I was panic-stricken. With her encouragement, I dared to think, "Hey, she's right. This is a piece of cake." On the regional level, I took third place. It wasn't a bad showing for my first time out, but I was nonetheless disappointed. Dottie reassured me that I was good; I just needed more practice. Success doesn't come easily. Dottie reminded me that I had only been involved with gymnastics for nine months as opposed to some of the other contestants, who had practiced it for three to five years. All in all, I did OK, she said.

That was all I needed to go on. At the next three regional meets, I placed first. And a year later, I took first place on the state level. The determination, perseverance and hard work finally paid off. I won, but I promise you, I wouldn't have done it without Dottie. Mentors can help you win in life.

Looking back now on the strength of balancing, I am able to transfer the need for life balance to current situations, and I am not afraid to fall. Look at life like a dance—full of movement, creativity, grace and balance.

WHEN WE NEED THE LESSONS, THE MENTORS APPEAR

There's an old saying that when the student is ready, the teacher is there. I believe the reverse of that also is true: when the teacher appears, the student is ready.

When interesting people appear in your life, ask yourself what lessons you might learn from them. Look into their character to determine what makes them interesting.

Sometimes, we pass through our lives and miss important cues. Often, we don't even recognize these cues until later in life, when we've had to learn something the hard way. Only in retrospect do we remember the cue that we either didn't recognize or chose to overlook.

Pay attention to the special people in your life. Learn from them. Emulate them, but don't lose yourself in the process. You are a unique being who attracts mentors as much as your mentors will attract you.

And when the two of you find each other, it can be the beginning of a wonderful relationship that you'll never forget—the kind that helps make building our roads a meaningful experience.

For now, let me serve as your mentor as you turn to the next chapter, where I'll tell you about the real magic generated by self-defined success, and how it can make you a dynamic road builder.

10

Magic of Self-Defined Success

When love and skill work together, expect
a masterpiece.

—JOHN RUSKIN

There's an episode of the old ''Twilight Zone'' series
that had quite an impact on me, and I'd like to share it
with you. At the beginning of the drama, police had
surrounded a notorious gangster, who opted to make a
last stand, rather than surrender. He was shot and killed.

The next thing the gangster realized he was regaining
consciousness in a brightly lit, expensive hotel suite. A
kindly, white-haired, white-bearded gentleman clad in a
white suit was standing over him. The gentleman explained that the gangster had passed on to the hereafter,
and that the gentleman was there to fulfill the gangster's
every wish.

The gangster was incredulous, but the kindly gentleman was as good as his word. The gangster asked for a
fine dinner, which the gentleman provided. Then he re-
quested female companionship. The gentleman arranged
to have the gangster provided with not one, but two sexy
women.

You've heard the old expression, ''I feel like I've died

and gone to heaven.'' This is exactly how the gangster felt. He was confused, however, because he had always assumed that people who had lived as he had—stealing, robbing and killing—didn't make it to heaven. But he didn't waste too much time thinking about that. After all, there were more things that he wanted.

He asked the gentleman to arrange for him to play roulette—and win. No sooner said than done. The gentleman led the gangster downstairs to the first floor of the hotel, where a roulette table and a crowd of gamblers awaited. Every number the gangster called came up a winner. By the end of the night, the gangster held more money in his hands than he had ever acquired in life.

This abundant lifestyle continued for several weeks. But the joy of success without effort steadily declined, until it reached the point when there was no satisfaction at all. The gangster became depressed. His kindly gentleman companion was most sensitive to his condition and, as always, was johnny-on-the-spot to offer his assistance.

''What's wrong?'' the gentleman asked. ''What can I do for you that I haven't already done?''

''Nothing,'' the gangster replied. ''I'm bored.''

''Let me know what I can do, and it shall be done,'' the gentleman volunteered. ''I'm here to serve your every need.''

''That's exactly the problem,'' the gangster snapped. ''I have enjoyed exquisite living quarters, gourmet dinners, beautiful women, winning at roulette . . . Anything and everything I want, you arrange for me to have. I don't have to lift a finger. There's no challenge here.''

''That's the way it is in the hereafter,'' the gentleman

explained. "Anything you want, I will provide—forever."

"But I don't want it to be that way," the gangster protested. "In life, I was a criminal, but even crime is work. I robbed and stole what I got. I ran risks and took chances. Sometimes, I lost, and I went to prison. But when I succeeded, success was sweet. Life wasn't a bed of roses, but it was interesting because it offered challenge. If there's no challenge here, I'm leaving. I'd rather be in the other place."

The gangster walked to the doors of the suite. But they were locked. He struggled with the handles, but they wouldn't budge. He turned to look at the gentleman, who now didn't appear very kindly at all. Instead, he sported a wicked grin and a malevolent glare.

"I beg your pardon," the gentleman said sharply. "This is 'the other place!'"

I don't know how sound the theology of that fable is, but it certainly makes a vital point.

WITHOUT CHALLENGE, LIFE WOULD BE A LIVING HELL

Think about how life would be if all of your wishes were granted as quickly as you made them, without any effort on your part. Just the mere thought of the idea might seem appealing. But if you were actually faced with the situation, as the gangster was, you might realize how much you really wouldn't appreciate it at all.

For example, you'd never have to go to work, because you could have all the money you wanted. You'd never have to do chores or run errands to keep the household operating smoothly, because you'd have servants taking care of those activities. You could have all the "toys" that you wanted, experience all the entertainment you desired and take as many vacations as you liked. And there would be nowhere in the world you couldn't go, as often as you wanted.

What then? After you got tired of having and doing it all, what would motivate you to get out of bed every day? Once you've enjoyed it all, what's left? Nothing! You'd be at the end of your emotional road—a dead-end much like the late billionaire Howard Hughes reportedly reached at the end of his life. If your every desire were fulfilled, you eventually would reach the point when you enjoyed absolutely nothing—just like the gangster discovered in the hell he initially mistook for heaven.

Relax. I don't think any of us are going to be plagued with this problem. Life doesn't reward anyone for merely wishing. Without a wealthy benefactor whose prime interest is fulfilling our desires, we'll have to work for what we want out of life. And that's the way it should be. When rewards come as a result of efforts—ideally honest efforts—we develop the desire to expend more effort so we can enjoy more rewards. That's what motivates most people to get out of bed every day.

THE CORNUCOPIA COMPLEX

Unfortunately, there are plenty of people who haven't quite caught on to this concept. Their development has been stunted, if not ruined, by the cornucopia complex.

A cornucopia is a symbol of abundance, affluence,

comfort and prosperity. It's image comes from the mythical overflowing "horn of plenty," the traditional symbol of a bountiful harvest. The cornucopia complex has been defined by Bruce A. Baldwin, author of *The Cornucopia Kids*, as "the expectation, based on years of experience in the home, that the good life will always be available for the asking, without effort and without the need for personal accountability."

In the economically growing environment of the 1950's and 1960's, adolescents in America were taught by parents to earn their privileges and allowances. The parents had weathered the lean years of the Great Depression and World War II rationing. Now, these adolescents are parents who have children of their own, and many of these children aren't being taught those lessons. Instead, these children are learning how to be manipulative, controlling and—worst of all—personally ineffective.

All people of all ages and of all cultures are primarily concerned with one goal—"How can I get what I want?" In the past, most people in our society came to learn (some sooner than others) that they could best generate positive results through their own efforts—by working productively to achieve their goals. Children of the past often learned this from a combination of parental guidance and their current circumstances. For example, during the Depression years, relatively few children received anything that wasn't an absolute necessity—let alone everything they wanted. As the depression eased, America entered World War II. Although most people were in a better financial situation, wartime rationing forced citizens to continue making a little go a long way.

Since World War II, however, Americans have enjoyed a relatively strong economic standing. People who had long sacrificed were ready to enjoy "the good life"—as well they should have. When the war ended, American industry finally had access to sufficient resources to make sure supply met demand. And with the onset of the "baby boom" era, America became the land of consumers. Depression-era children were now prosperous parents, who wanted to give their children the things they didn't have or had to work hard to get.

Although it can be argued that this "cornucopia complex" actually began during the 1950's, I believe that the complex is worse today. Baby boomers are rearing their children during an even more affluent age, which offers a wider variety and greater selection of "toys" and status symbols than any period in history!

CHILDREN LEARN WHAT THEIR PARENTS TEACH THEM

When the demands of children are routinely satisfied— when they can get what they want without expending productive effort—they learn that they can get what they want merely by making demands. Parents who acquiesce to these demands are teaching this lesson.

Meanwhile, consider the case of the children who have grown up with such an attitude. Aren't they a great deal like the gangster? Having learned that they can get whatever they want by asking or demanding, is it at all surprising that they find themselves bored most of the time? They have developed no purpose in life, because they have never needed one. There is nothing to motivate them to take productive action, because they've learned that rewards come without challenge. As a result, there is nothing for which they can develop enthusiasm, or a passion that makes human existence tolerable.

We can track this decline in enthusiasm over the generations. During the depression, people were enthusiastic about working. Jobs were scarce, and so was money. During this financially bleak period, one of the most exciting things in the world was to have a job. It didn't matter what kind of work the job involved. Any job that offered a paycheck, no matter how small, was valued. In those days of high unemployment, working was a privilege.

Two and three decades later, the baby boomers were born into a world of career opportunity, higher education and a work ethic instilled by a generation of parents who had endured the depression. These children often held part-time jobs and sometimes applied their money toward cars, clothing and education—if not toward the support of the family unit itself.

Now the baby boomers are parents, who are giving their children even more than they got. But, all too often, the children aren't required to expend effort to get it. That might be one reason that fast-food chains like McDonald's, Burger King and Domino's Pizza are hiring senior citizens—the Depression era youth, still willing to work after all these years—because today's youth won't even consider sleeping for minimum wage. And, to play the devil's advocate, if modern-day teens have learned they can get more money through an easier method—i.e., haranguing their parents—why should they settle for less?

THE REAL WORLD IS THE BEST TEACHER

Of course, all parties must end eventually. What will happen to these children when they become adults and enter the real world? Having never learned to be productive, or to develop the enthusiasm and motivation that goes with productivity, today's young people have several choices of roads to build. They can overcome years of negative conditioning by being willing to face reality—to gain first-hand life experience. Many of them will do just that, although it's likely to be a long, uphill climb. But others will settle for nondemanding jobs that offer just enough compensation for them to eat and pay rent. With a past devoid of challenge, they'll continue to avoid it. Some will find themselves emotionally immobilized to the point that qualifying for welfare is the only way they'll be able to survive.

I'll give you an example of what I'm talking about. I know a woman whose son is an extremely bright young man. Sean and his mother had talked frequently about career choices, college and success, including what success requires and what a person can and cannot expect from it. Sean had given his mother the impression of "having it all together," or being a person who, for the most part, would not make any decisions without first giving them serious thought.

One day, Sean came racing into the kitchen and proclaimed with great enthusiasm, "I have decided what I am going to do." Then he announced that he had chosen which college to attend. First, it was a college that specialized in engineering, rather than the liberal arts for which Sean showed most interest and was best suited. And, second, tuition at that particular school was astronomically high.

When Sean's mother stated her reservations to her son, Sean replied, "Yeah, but all of my friends are gonna go there, too. What a blast! And the best part is this—all you have to do is give me $40,000, and I am on my way!"

For an instant, Sean's mother toyed with the idea of hanging her son by his thumbs. But she kept her cool. "Sean, do you know how long it takes your father and me to earn $40,000?" she asked. "That's a lot of money!"

"Well, we're rich, aren't we?" Sean countered. "You're working, and Dad's working. You guys are responsible for me! You are always telling me that! If you really care about me, you will give me the money."

With that, Sean stormed out of the house wearing his Reebok sneakers, Guess jeans and designer T-shirt. Once outside, he jumped into the car he had received as a high-school graduation gift and drove away.

As it turned out, Sean did not get the tuition money from his parents. In fact, when he was informed by his father that he would be responsible for raising half of his tuition, Sean abruptly dropped his plans to attend college. Instead, he got a job filling vending machines, because "it's easy," he said.

Sean's next step was to move out on his own because house rules and regulations had become too stringent to suit him. Of course, he left with his waterbed, stereo system and color television set. He was lucky to leave with his life after he suggested taking along the family room furniture.

I guess that's why Sol Gordon, an expert on teen behavior (if there really is such an animal), advises parents not to have teenagers unless they have a sense of humor. Otherwise, they might find themselves serving time for murder.

SELF-DEFINED SUCCESS MIGHT NOT BE "HEAVEN," BUT IT'S A FAR CRY FROM "HELL"

Believe me, I'm not condoning the fabled gangster's chosen lifestyle. But at least he, unlike many teens, had one right idea about life. He had defined his own success and was willing to build his road leading to it. There was nothing wrong with his vision of success—being wealthy and living the good life. Certainly, his choice of means was unethical. But his concept—define your own success and define your own rules—was right on target.

I don't know how you're faring on the construction of your life road. I don't know if you're happy, miserable or at some point in-between. I don't know how you feel about your career, your social life, your relationships with others and your prospects for the future. In short, I don't know anything about your life and lifestyle, your responsibilities and the things you do everyday to fulfill them.

But I do know there is only one thing that you absolutely "must" do. One day, you must die. There is no way around it. Medical science might add 50 years to average lifespans, but the fact remains that one day, life must end. Until that day, you will live. (Even suicide can't relieve you of these responsibilities.)

Other than that, anything else you want to do is entirely up to you.

That's right. You're building your own road, remember? If you choose to use some of your income to support your ailing parents, that's your choice. If you'd rather gamble it away on roulette, it's your decision. You don't have to pay your debts if you don't mind having a poor credit rating. You don't even have to support your children; you don't have to work, get married, fall in love or own a home. You don't have to do anything. It's your choice.

You get the picture, I'm sure. There's no law that says you can't quit showing up for work, stay out all night or satisfy a spur-of-the-moment urge to hitchhike across the country, as long as you're willing to accept the consequences.

The only date you unquestionably must keep is the one you have with the Supreme Commissioner of Highways. Despite the oft-described inevitability of taxes, you don't even "have to" pay them, if you'd prefer to go to prison, assume another identity or hide from the law for the rest of your life. For as long as you live, the only thing you absolutely, positively and definitely "must" do is die.

So in the meantime, why not live it up? Do what you want to do—find your own happiness. Do it now! That's exactly what you do when you pursue self-defined success. We travel the routes of our choice. We do with our lives what we'd like and pursue our dreams. That alone is the reward in itself. Bringing a reality to our vision is our success.

SELF-DEFINED SUCCESS OFFERS HOPE

If the gangster had exercised genuine vision, he might have chosen another career. History has proven that gangsters who aren't brought to justice generally meet with untimely, violent ends. But he chose his road for the same reason we choose ours.

Self-defined success, regardless of how it's identified, offers us the encouragement of hope. The gangster had hope that he could get away with his crimes, right up until the very end. When we live the lives we choose, we have hope that we'll achieve the success we envision.

Hope is part of the magic of self-defined success. If we work jobs devoid of fulfillment, we eliminate hope. We merely trade our labors for paychecks, and we usually feel short-changed for the trouble. However, when we do work that fulfills us, receiving pay for it is sometimes secondary. Ask yourself this question: ''Would I do what I do for free?'' If the answer is yes, you can bet you are on the right road.

Hope isn't the only quality that self-defined success generates. There's real magic in pursuing self-defined success because it generates other productive qualities that the gangster in hell will never experience.

1. Motivation. If your house was struck by lightning and started to burn, I'll bet you'd be motivated to get out quickly! That's an example of how self-defined success leads to motivation. Your desire to stay alive inspires you to find the fastest route to safety. When we define our own success and the rewards we will receive, we can't help but become motivated to achieve them. And if we're not motivated, then perhaps we've defined the wrong success. If that's the case, we might need to rethink the courses of our roads.

2. Enthusiasm. It's difficult to be motivated without being enthusiastic. In the case that your house is set ablaze, would you not be enthusiastic about exiting to safety? If not, then your life must not be worth much to you. The absence of enthusiasm in any endeavor means you can take or leave success or failure. If that's the way you feel about anything that plays a significant role in your life, then you might consider finding something else to do. Ralph Waldo Emerson said, "Nothing great was ever achieved without enthusiasm."

3. Drive and energy. Even if you were awakened from a deep sleep to discover your house alight, I'll bet you would develop boundless drive and energy to get out. When you pursue self-defined success, it's amazing how much personal power you can develop. It's as if the need to succeed overpowers all other needs. You'll become truly dynamic.

4. Commitment. With your house on its way to becoming ashes—and you with it, if you don't get out—wouldn't you be committed to find an escape route? You wouldn't take time to fix a midnight snack, check out what's on television or even answer a ringing telephone if you were truly committed to saving yourself. People don't succeed when they allow themselves to be sidetracked too frequently. They postpone doing the things that will lead to the achievement of their goals. But with commitment, you can avoid this trap. Commitment helps you focus on your goals, which helps you avoid being sidetracked.

There's real magic in self-defined success. If there is anything wrong with the world today, perhaps its the fact that a majority of the people aren't pursuing their own ideas of success.

If the world needs to be changed, maybe it can be, if each of us would take the time to define our idea of success and expend the effort to pursue it.

If you haven't defined your own success, why not do it? Although it might take you a while to achieve your goal, you can benefit immediately from the magic offered by the pursuit. You'll become a better person, and you'll be taking a giant step toward changing the world by changing yourself.

If you start building your own road, realize that it's a lifetime commitment. Roadbuilding is a job that's never finished. I'll talk more about this in the next chapter.

11

Road Building Is Never Finished

Failure is not fatal; victory is not success.
—Tony Richardson

The road we travel is not finished until the Supreme Commissioner of Highways calls a halt to our construction.

Even if we achieve the destination of our wildest dreams, our roads go on. Even if we become so discouraged that we're tempted to stop building toward our chosen destination, we'll continue to build in some direction. As long as we breathe, we build our roads.

The purpose of road building, of course, is to reach our destinations, to collect the rewards and experience the victory of achievement. But victory is a funny thing. The thrill of it is fleeting. People who think achieving any single goal—no matter how significant—will allow them to live happily and fulfilled ever after have a lot to learn about life.

Fortunately, the same is true with defeat. It hurts, but it, too, is fleeting. Its misery and disappointment won't last forever. People who believe that a single defeat spells the end of a road in their chosen direction most often live to learn otherwise.

Sometimes, life has a way of kicking us in the teeth at times when we can least deal with the blow. A valued relationship, job or way of life comes to an end, and we're left to pick up the pieces from the emotional wreckage. Our accustomed props and crutches have been kicked out from under us, and we feel devalued.

But we really haven't been devalued. Each of us is valuable, separate and apart from anything we do or any role we play. When we lose something we value, such as a job, relationship or way of life, we hurt because we'll miss the satisfaction we received from it. We might also feel pain because we've become accustomed to enjoying our worth to someone else, and now we no longer feel needed. When we lose a job, we mourn the loss of our worth to our employer. When we lose a relationship, we grieve over the loss of our worth to another person.

No one likes to lose, or be rejected. But the loss or rejection doesn't make us any less worthy to be happy and fulfilled. We are unique, valuable individuals. And because we have value, we can continue to build more road and develop more worthwhile relationships, jobs or ways of life.

PAIN YIELDS STRENGTH

Still, it takes time to get over the hurt. Let's be realistic. I could write you a flowery passage about how, if we really had our self-esteem intact, we could weather our losses without pain. I've known some people who could do just that—at least seemingly so.

People who act as if significant losses don't affect them are only fooling themselves. They don't have to stage a histrionic scene or go into a depression for months. But hurting is simply a sign that something we lost was important to us. It's all right to hurt when we lose something of value; it's even all right to demonstrate that hurt.

And there's good news about hurting. Although it feels bad, it eventually makes us strong. Once we've experienced a hurt, a similar occurrence in the future won't hurt as badly because we've "been through it" before. Also, hurting broadens our character. It tests and even develops our inner resources, because, like it or not, we're forced to cope with our pain. And, third, hurting makes us wise. When a situation causes us pain, we'll be more likely to avoid a similar situation in the future. It's like the conversation between the patient and the doctor. The patient raises his hand and says, "Doc, it only hurts when I do this," and the doctor advises, "Well, don't do that!"

Physical pain is a natural response to injury. When any part of our anatomy is injured, the resulting pain warns us to protect the painful area so it can heal properly in minimal time. Perhaps when we hurt emotionally, our inner pain tells us to protect our emotions from additional anguish so they can work things out in a calm environment. It's nature at work.

When you experience problems, look within and look to nature. Nature solves her own problems. Take a tree for example. In the spring, the tree buds, revealing its potential which is realized in the summer when deep, green leaves abound. The leaves provide beauty, shade and even oxygen through the process of photosynthesis. That's quite a contribution. Then it seems that just when we start to take the leaves for granted, they change into brilliant colors, again commanding our attention. But at this point, photosynthesis ceases. The leaves produce no more oxygen, and the tree's shade potential and beauty diminish steadily as the leaves slowly fall to the ground, bringing a very dramatic close to the tree's annual cycle. Next winter arrives, causing the tree to enter a period of dormancy before the growth cycle repeats itself.

Sometimes, our lives follow a similar type of cycle when we undertake new endeavors, relationships or ways of life. We bud, or show our potential. When our potential is developed, we can provide beauty, service or pleasure, much like the tree in summer.

When our props or crutches are taken away, we are much like the trees in autumn and winter. Sometimes, it's necessary to take a dramatic turn and change directions or even disappear from the scene for a time of reflection—a time for planning new growth. But after a period of replenishing, we come back just as strong, if not stronger, than before, like the new leaves of spring.

I'LL BE BACK, JACK!

The reason we can recover from our disappointments and losses is because we're resilient. Sure, we get hurt. But we heal. If we weren't resilient, we'd never survive our first puppy loves. Remember how painful yours was at the time? Although you might have thought then that you'd never recover, you did. In retrospect, you're probably glad the relationship went sour or never developed, because it was the first in a series of relationships that helped you build character and maturity.

It's the same way with jobs. Many people who have

been subjected to the painful, debilitating experience of having been discharged from their jobs often discover later that the firing was a critical factor that led to their moving on to greener pastures.

Likewise with disappointments. In the early 20th century, a young, struggling actor declined the opportunity to invest several hundred dollars into a gold mining effort. The venture proved lucrative. Had he invested, the actor could have become a millionaire. Since he didn't, he was forced to continue working as an actor—a venture that proved extremely successful and fulfilling for him. The actor was Boris Karloff, who achieved overnight fame when cast as the monster in the classic 1931 film version of Mary Shelley's *Frankenstein*. He later was quoted as saying he was glad he didn't invest in the gold mine, because the easy financial success might have prevented him from making anything of himself.

When life's losses and disappointments knock us down, or when other people use us as stepping stones to get ahead, it's easy to let the pain and hurt get the best of us. But we can keep pain to a minimum by remembering that we are resilient, and that a better day awaits us if we are willing to continue building our roads in our chosen direction.

To sum it up in four words: "I'll be back, Jack!" That's my motto, and it's gotten me through a host of personal losses. Looking back, each one helped me to become stronger and better prepared to tend to the business of building my road. And when all was said and done, I wound up with better career situations, better ways of life and better relationships than those I had lost.

Form your own motto to help you weather tough times.

I'll never forget a woman who attended one of my seminars. When I asked participants to share their mottos with me, the woman said, "My motto is, 'If I live through this, it will be the best experience I have ever had.'" We all laughed at the time. Yet, when you think about it—my friend is right.

I'll be back, Jack! It's a matter of attitude. When you lose, your life isn't over. It's probably just beginning. If you let your loss defeat you, you might lose yourself, or commit emotional suicide. If that happens, you'll have no one to blame but yourself.

Don't lose yourself for anyone or anything. Hang tough when you have an *emotional* fall, and you will bounce back even higher than before.

VALUE JUDGING HINDERS HEALING

Emotional setbacks result from disappointments with others or, in some cases, ourselves. When we lose jobs, ways of life, friends, lovers or spouses, it's often easy to get lost in trying to figure out what went wrong, and why.

Certainly, it's beneficial to learn from our mistakes, so we won't repeat them. Beyond that, additional analysis is not only unproductive, it's counterproductive. When others disappoint us for whatever reason, why waste time trying to second-guess their reasons? Placing a motive on an action is called value judging, and all the value judging in the world won't change the fact that we've been disappointed.

Or, perhaps I should say, value judging won't change the fact that we've allowed others to disappoint us. When we grieve over a disappointment with another, aren't we really disheartened because we have created an image of someone else that isn't consistent with his or her behavior? People we choose not to like cannot disappoint us because we don't expect kindness from them. It's only the people we believe to be our friends who disappoint us.

It doesn't matter why people disappoint us. The fact that they do is enough for us to determine our next move. Sometimes, inaction is the best course of action. People aren't perfect, and we will occasionally disappoint others and be disappointed. Many times, people unintentionally disappoint each other without even being aware of it. Perhaps their actions were thoughtless, but no malice was intended. Yet, when we indulge in harsh value judging, we often attach to another's behavior non-existent motives that have the ability to generate real resentment and ill will. On the other hand, when we value judge naively to create suitable excuses for someone else's offensive behavior, we might be making concessions to maintain a relationship that we really need to let go.

It's a good policy to overlook occasional disappointments. Of course, each disappointment should be weighed on its own merit. But in many cases, to end an otherwise fulfilling relationship because of a single disappointment might be comparable to cutting off your nose to spite your face.

When disappointment becomes a way of life in a relationship, perhaps we need to remember the tree in autumn. We may need to withdraw and plan for a period of new growth. All we need to know to make such a decision is that we do not like the way we are being treated. It's not necessary to analyze why we're being treated that way. A good question to ask is, "Why am I allowing myself to be treated this way?"

It reminds me of the Peanuts comic strip. Lucy Van Pelt is forever inviting Charlie Brown to kick a football that she holds for him. And each time, Charlie Brown spends a few minutes second-guessing whether or not Lucy will pull the ball away at the last critical second, causing him to fall flat on his back. Yet, he always rationalizes that she won't, and he takes a running start for the ball. And, of course, she always pulls the ball away. If Charlie Brown did less value judging, he'd learn his lesson, and he would stop falling for the gag—no pun intended.

If someone slaps you across the face each time the two of you encounter, is it important for you to understand why you're being slapped before you decide that you'd better keep a safe distance? Don't waste energy value judging. Save the energy for developing new relationships.

CHANGE IS THE ONLY THING WE CAN COUNT ON

Although the loss of our props and crutches hurts, it is precisely those losses that help us build character and strength. And if we are to continue to grow, there is no way to build our roads around the pain of periodic loss and disappointment. For example, a star high school athlete might experience depression upon graduation, when he or she is forced to relinquish the star role. The only way he or she could have avoided the loss is by not having gotten involved with athletics at all. Valued friends might leave our lives when their jobs take them to another part of the country. We could have avoided the pain by refusing to make friends. The loss of a job not only might deprive us of valued career status, but also of an accustomed lifestyle that the job's income helped make possible. Of course, we could have avoided that hurt by not taking the job in the first place.

Nothing ever stays the same for long. Things can change to suit us, or they can change to disappoint us. But they will change. And if we're serious about building our roads to our chosen destinations, we'd better be prepared for the possibility of change in all areas of our lives.

Of course, we often don't know when situations beyond our control will change. So the best way to be prepared for change is to be prepared to change ourselves. It has been said that there are three ways to effect personal change.

1 Shock. This is the fastest method of change. Anything that shocks our system might lead to change. A heart attack might motivate us to adopt a more healthy lifestyle. A divorce might motivate us to take a hard look at what we did to contribute to it and change our behavior. Of course, there's a disadvantage to shock-induced change: we usually suffer some degree of damage. And, sometimes, it's irreparable.

2 Adaptation. This is a more common method of change, but it's the slowest. We adapt as our circumstances change. We change our spending habits to accommodate changes in income. We change our opinions of others and the way we treat them as they change the way they treat us. We change our values as we get older and learn more about life.

When we change by adapting, we don't prepare for circumstances. Instead, we allow them to dictate the courses of our lives. Sometimes, the results can be unfavorable. For example, if you put a frog into a pan of hot water, it will jump out. But if you put it in a pan of cold water, it will remain there, even if the pan is placed upon a burner that is gradually increasing the temperature of the water. The frog will adapt to the higher temperatures—until it is boiled to death.

For a historical example, British Prime Minister Neville Chamberlain in 1938 sought to avoid war in Europe by acquiescing to Adolph Hitler's demands to claim Czechoslovakia. Both England and France, allies to Czechoslovakia, authorized the transfer of that country's border areas to Nazi Germany in what is known as the Munich Agreement, which Chamberlain touted as the pact to ensure "peace for our time." England and France "sold out" Czechoslovakia to adapt to the desires of the Nazis. But it still didn't avert World War II, which broke out the next year. Chamberlain's popularity was in shambles, and he was replaced in 1940 by Winston Churchill, whose policy was to settle for nothing short of an Allied forces victory.

3 Voluntary change. This is the best—and most difficult—method to effect personal change, since it offers neither the startling impetus of shock, nor the ease of adaptation. Generally, voluntary change takes longer to effect than shock-induced change, but it avoids the damage. And voluntary change is faster and offers better results than adaptation, or change by necessity. We assess ourselves and our situations, determine that a change might lead to a more favorable situation, then we make the change. Sometimes, it requires letting go of a current job, relationship or lifestyle while we pursue another that we perceive to be more rewarding. Usually, voluntary change requires more will power than the other two methods, and it involves some degree of risk. But remember, nothing significant is obtained without risk.

No matter how we choose to change, dealing with change means giving up something for something else. Usually, it's more difficult to give up an accustomed job, relationship or way of life through voluntary change than it is through shock-induced change or adaptation. But the rewards on the whole are better, because we're in the best position to effect positive change in our lives.

Change is one thing we can always count on. We can view it from a negative perspective (giving something away) or from a positive perspective (getting or adding to what we already have). The choice is up to you.

Let me offer an example. Businesses differ in their willingness to accept technology. There are the pioneers, who are willing to invest in the newest products on the market. They know that almost any device that can save time and effort can pay for itself. They don't mind changing the status quo for the possibility of creating more profitable situations for themselves. But pioneers take financial risks, because not all new technology survives. For example, think of the people who invested in the beta-format videocassette recorders, which are virtually obsolete now.

Then there are business people who won't invest in any technology until they are absolutely convinced it will be profitable and that the system is here to stay. These businesses "play it safe" by adapting to conditions. On the down side, they don't stand to profit as much as the pioneers, who invested in the technology at the earliest opportunity.

Finally, we have the business people who won't invest in new technology until it's evident that it's the key to survival. The shock of impending financial doom wakes them up—but, sometimes, the awakening is too late to head off the inevitable disaster.

I'm not advocating change for the sake of change. As they say, "If it ain't broke, don't fix it." But it's not a bad idea to apply vision and foresight to our personal situations to determine whether voluntary changes can improve them. If so, it's usually better to change willingly, rather than run the risk of adapting too late to achieve optimum results or, worse yet, receiving a shock that can injure or kill us.

THE ROAD ENDS, BUILD MORE ROAD

When the valued props and crutches are knocked out from under us and it appears that our roads are at end, what do we do? What do we do when a valued job, relationship or lifestyle disintegrates, and the roads we've built leading to them reach dead ends?

Simple. We build more road. Life goes on. We choose a new direction, and build our roads with dignity. We don't moan, groan or indulge in sob stories. Wallowing in misery does nothing positive to improve our situations. Indulgence in sorrow eventually chases away our friends, who have better things to do than listen to us rehash our miseries. And dwelling on misfortunes actually prolongs the agony. It's best to put the past behind us and move on. With enough time and distance, the disappointments might even be humorous in retrospect.

Think about it. Anything we find amusing would really not be funny at all if we viewed it seriously. Although we might initially laugh if we saw a busboy trip and drop a tray of dishes, shattering them to pieces, how humorous would it be if we stopped to think that he might be charged for the damage or even discharged for his clumsiness?

By the same token, humor results when a misfortune is viewed with objectivity. One day, three of us went for a boat ride in an aluminum rowboat with an outboard motor. As we glided around the perimeter of the lake, I noticed the motor had caught fire. I yelled to the others. I was terrified. I didn't want to burn, but I didn't want to jump overboard, because I do not swim.

By the time I developed the presence of mind to realize I was wearing a life preserver, I noticed the flames growing bigger. But I also noticed gasoline in the water. I was so panic stricken that I couldn't decide whether to jump in the water or stay put. When I realized that the motor might explode and spurt flaming gasoline all over me, I decided to take the plunge. So I jumped into the water to make my way to shore, which was about 100 yards away.

As it turned out, I didn't really need the life preserver.

The water was only four feet deep. The fire was extinguished almost simultaneously. As I walked to the shore, my friends were laughing hysterically. It wasn't until I reached the shore that I decided that the whole thing was really funny.

When we can laugh at our misfortunes, we have truly survived them. And when we can laugh, we're often in the best position to learn, because it shows that we're not taking ourselves seriously. And perhaps that's the best advice for building a road.

The late actor Spencer Tracy often advised young actors, "Take your profession seriously, and yourself not one whit." And noted comedian Red Skelton once said, "Never take life seriously, because you'll never get out of it alive."

WE CAN ALWAYS TOP OURSELVES

Perhaps a good basis to use for effecting personal change is to use our past successes as gauges. No matter how much success we've enjoyed in the past, we can always be better. Perfection is a state that cannot be improved, and human beings aren't perfect. So we can always work to improve ourselves. Our next success can always be better than our previous one.

People who live long, productive lives adhere to that philosophy. Success gives them a taste for more success, and they continue to build their roads in the directions of their choice. And don't forget the magic of self-defined success. The drive, energy and enthusiasm it generates can't help but add years to our lives. On the other hand, it seems that the saddest people in life are those who have enjoyed success in the past and are still clinging to the memory. Society labels them as "has-beens." No telling where their roads are going to go. These are the people I encourage to remember that if they experience just one success, they can experience another. Success is repeatable.

No matter how significant our success might be, we can always strive to achieve better. If we must keep building our roads—and we must—then it's worth our effort to choose the direction in which we build them.

No matter in what field of endeavor you aspire to excel, you'll need good leadership to reach your destination. And you are the perfect person for the job, since only you know exactly where you're going. Self-directed leadership is essential to building good roads. You can derive great benefit by learning the basic principles of self-directed leadership. The next chapter of this book will acquaint you with these principles and show you how to employ them while building your road.

III

LEADING YOURSELF
AND OTHERS

12

The Art of Self-Directed Leadership

There's only one corner of the universe you can be certain of improving; that's your own self.

—ALDOUS HUXLEY

In real life, highway construction crews can go back and tear up defective roads they've built, then repave them. They can even change a road's course by straightening curves or eliminating turns if the original design doesn't provide for the smooth, safe flow of traffic. But when it comes to constructing our life roads, once the course is set and the road is built, it's history. So you'll want to be certain that you build your road correctly the first time.

Why is it so important that we get our roads right the first time? After all, barring accident or illness, we'll probably have enough time to correct any mistakes we make, right? Who knows how much time we have left to reach our destinations? Anyway, that's not the point.

Before starting construction on the road leading to your chosen destination, it's vital to realize that important people will be watching you. These are people who will be concerned with your past road, your current road and the direction of your future road.

Who are these people? They can be anyone. They can be potential friends, potential employers, potential spouses, potential business partners, potential clients—even potential proteges, or people who would look to you to be their mentor.

These people might serve different needs in our lives. But to give them a common bond, these people will be interested in the possibility of at least intersecting their roads with ours. They might consider designing their roads to weave frequently in and out of ours, as would potential friends. Or they might contemplate working with us to build our roads, if they are considering us as potential spouses, employees or business partners.

These people will base their decisions to get involved with the building of your road on two factors. First, they won't even consider joining you in construction unless they believe you'll build your future road to coincide with theirs. And, second, the only way they can predict the course of your future road is by looking at the road that's already behind you.

Of course, we all make mistakes in the building of our roads—flaws that we would later like to be able to reconstruct. Since we can't, we learn from our mistakes and go on. And all that really counts is that we go on in the right direction. It's the course of our roads, more than the actual roads, that others will look at to determine whether they want to get involved with helping in the construction.

How do we determine the direction of our roads? Obviously, we determine direction by establishing a destination. But it takes more than that. Many people set destinations they never come close to reaching because they allow themselves to get sidetracked along the way.

Once we've set a destination, how do we stay the course? We do it by following the principles of self-directed leadership. Only when others see that we can successfully lead ourselves will they choose to join us in building our own roads.

WHAT DO WE NEED TO SUCCEED?

What is the magic ingredient for success? Is it belief in ourselves and our abilities? Determination? Persistence? Dedication? Certainly, all those things are critical to succeeding in any endeavor we'd undertake. But there's still another vital ingredient to success. Without it, it's unlikely that we would succeed at anything.

The ingredient? Other people. Without them, we can only succeed at being hermits. Even if we undertake traditional solitary endeavors, such as body-building or self-education, it would be difficult to succeed without advice, encouragement and feedback.

It is doubtful that you can reach more complex goals without support from other people. Suppose you want to start your own business. Of course, you must be good at producing the goods or performing the services you have to offer. But you'll have to do more than that. You will need to conduct yourself and your trans-actions in such a manner that your customers or clients will enjoy doing business with you. Rarely can a business survive on onetime sales. Only if customers enjoy conducting business with you will they return. Of course, it goes without saying that you must be honest and dependable, and must provide good value. But it's also necessary to treat customers well.

Studies show that people regularly do business with organizations because they like the people who operate them. Research also shows that people stop doing business with an organization when they feel they've been mistreated. More importantly, studies indicate that customers who feel they have been treated unfavorably will not only stop patronizing the business, but will spread the bad news to their friends and acquaintances. If enough people decide they don't want to have anything to do with your business, you won't have a business for long.

The same rule applies to career advancement. You won't rise on any career ladder unless you are valued, trusted and respected by the people who have final say over which rung you occupy. If they don't want you to ascend, you won't. Again, you must be good at what you do. But even the best knowledge, skills and abilities won't allow you to rise very high unless you use your abilities to work well with your co-workers.

And this rule applies double with forming personal relationships. No matter how much you desire to be someone's friend, spouse or significant other, you won't achieve your goal unless you can appeal to that person on his or her terms. No matter how much you like someone else, the potential relationship will never develop if he or she doesn't value, trust and respect you.

Of course, we cannot control how others feel about us, but we can certainly design our actions and behavior to appeal to others. I'm not saying that we should try to be something that we aren't and run the risk of losing ourselves in the process. All I'm talking about is treating others with "courtesy-plus" and respect.

If you're not accustomed to doing that, make it a priority to start the very good habit. It will not only make reaching your destination more likely, but it will also make the trip more rewarding.

YOU'VE GOT TO BUILD A "CONSIDERATE" ROAD

Many otherwise-competent people fail to reach their destinations because they do not have good interpersonal interaction skills. Marriages fail, friendships disintegrate and jobs don't work out because people don't know how or won't treat others with courtesy and respect. Many arrogant executives have been frozen in their climb up the career ladder—if not knocked off—because they treated their subordinates as commodities to be used, instead of as people to be valued.

Subordinates are like customers. If they don't like the way they're being treated, they'll take their talents elsewhere. Even employers have competition. Managers and supervisors who don't value their subordinates invite increased levels of turnover within their businesses, which will result in decreased efficiency and productivity. The managers and supervisors must answer for this, as well they should.

But let's look at what happens with the subordinates

who choose to stay on, even though they feel they're being treated unfairly. It's only human nature that they will hold back in their production. Would you knock yourself out for someone who didn't appreciate it, if you could survive by doing less? Under such circumstances, overall efficiency will suffer, and the manager or supervisor again will find himself behind the eight ball.

We get back what we give, and we give back what we get. The Golden Rule—do unto others as you would have others do unto you—offers us as much benefit as it does others. When we treat people the way we'd like to be treated, we're likely to be treated that way in return.

But there's an even better rule—the Platinum Rule, which is "Do unto others as they would have you do unto them." When we treat people the way they would like to be treated, they will likely pay us the same courtesy. This is the secret behind smooth, interpersonal interaction which helps two or more people build smooth, straight roads to mutual destinations.

COMMUNICATION—THE KEY TO ALL RELATIONSHIPS

Regardless of the relationship, be it marriage, friendship, business associates or superior-subordinate, it will only be as good as the quality of communication between the parties.

When you think about it, a relationship is nothing at all without communication. The way we treat people is communication. When we treat them badly, we communicate contempt and ill will. When we value them, we communicate admiration and appreciation.

Sometimes, we communicate without uttering a sound. A smile, a nod of the head, a handshake, and an "OK" gesture often can communicate more than a thousand words. By the same token, a frown, a glare and a decidedly different type of gesture leaves no doubt as to what a person chooses not to say. Both messages are crystal clear, despite the fact that not a single word is spoken.

Even body language is a form of communication and an extremely powerful form at that. Some studies indicate that body language accounts for more than half of communication when we meet another person for the first time.

We are judged by many factors when we first meet someone. We tend to form immediate opinions of like and dislike based on any number of impressions. What are you communicating to the world? Is it a positive powerful personal presence? What message are you sending? Do you send a message of competence, intelligence, professional appearance and high self-esteem? If not, you're sending the wrong message.

The use of your personal power is found in your use of words, gestures, facial expressions or body language, and it is communicated in three different ways. The way you choose will determine how you treat others and, in all probability, the way others will treat you in return.

1 Aggressive. The person who communicates aggressively has little or no regard for the feelings of the other person. Messages generally are delivered in a "do-it-or-else" fashion. Bullies and supervisors who enjoy being "bosses" communicate aggressively. So do over-powering spouses, spoiled brats, some prison guards and all drill sergeants. People who must communicate with aggressive people usually don't like them. In aggressive communication, someone always loses power, dignity, respect or trust.

2 Non-assertive. The person who communicates non-assertively has little or no regard for his or her own feelings. As a result, the communicator will place utmost significance on the other person's feelings, even at the expense of his or her own. Who are people who communicate non-assertively? Generally, they are the perfect foils for aggressive people—anyone who is intimidated by others, including subordinates, spouses, prisoners and military recruits. Non-assertive communication effects a lose/win situation.

3 Assertive. People who communicate assertively speak up for their rights without infringing on the rights of others. Assertive messages are honest, but they are delivered with respect. This doesn't mean that others necessarily have to like hearing assertive messages. People who communicate assertively have high self-esteem. They don't need to malign or belittle others, but they refuse to allow others to take advantage of them. Assertive communication effects a win/win situation.

It has been said that what we say has a relatively insignificant impact compared to the impact of the way we say it. People have feelings. Even if people do something to anger you, it's better to explain in a forthright manner why you are angry instead of putting them down or questioning their heritage.

PRECISE COMMUNICATION STRENGTHENS RELATIONSHIPS

It is important to be assertive when building relationships based on mutual trust and respect. But to build strong, effective relationships, it's vital to be precise when communicating. You might have heard it said that a vital ingredient to a successful marriage is good communication. Actually, this is true for any relationship. When people do not communicate well, it is easy for their relationship to go sour.

Let's take a look at some reasons that communication goes awry.

1 Lack of information. When communication fails, lack of vital information is perhaps the most common reason. For example, a physician might prescribe medicine to cure a sickness. If it's essential that the drug be taken on a full stomach—and the physician fails to convey that message—the patient might take the medication before meals and develop a raucous case of nausea. The underlying cause? Poor communication.

2 Making incorrect assumptions. The speaker assumes that the listener knows certain facts, and phrases the message based on those assumptions. For example, a mechanic informs a customer to add water periodically to the car's faulty radiator to protect the engine. If the mechanic incorrectly assumes that the customer knows that (to avoid cracking the engine block) the engine must be operating while water is added, the customer might ruin the engine, which is precisely the outcome he or she is trying to prevent.

3 Wrong choice of words. This is another common reason communication goes astray. Often in a search for appropriate words, we make poor choices. We might know what we mean to say, but the listener knows only what he or she hears. If we tell someone to pick up some salt at the market, but we meant to say ''sugar'' instead, we can't blame the listener for following our directions.

4 Words with multiple meanings. Suppose someone brought a donkey onto your front lawn. And, suppose that upon discovering the animal, you ordered the person to get his or her donkey off your property. If you chose to use a three-letter synonym for ''donkey,'' you might have a fight on your hands. Of course, this is an unlikely scenario, but it illustrates the point. It has been estimated that the most common 500 words of the English language have a total of 14,000 definitions—an average of 28 definitions per word. When we use words with multiple meanings, we should be sure to be precise in our communication.

5 Slang. Grass is something we mow. In drug lingo, it's something you smoke. If we're in a hurry for a hamburger, we might tell the waiter to ''step on it.'' If the waiter takes us seriously, we might receive a squashed hamburger. One of my colleagues, noted speaker Nido Qubein, came to the United States in the mid-1960's.

His knowledge of the English language was limited. He often talks about making transactions at area businesses. When the cashier thanked him for his patronage and said, "Come back!"—meaning that he or she would appreciate repeat business—Nido took the remark literally. He would walk back to the cashier and ask, "What do you want?" Be careful when using slang.

Poor communication isn't always the fault of the speaker. Sometimes, the listener must accept the responsibility. Here are some reasons that communication breaks down on the listener's level.

1 Being closed-minded. When a speaker delivers a message that is contrary to our beliefs and values, we might reject the message altogether. Closed-minded people often fail to learn things that could help them develop greater effectiveness—and humility.

2 Inattention. When a speaker discusses a subject that we perceive to be too complicated or boring to understand, we often let the speaker talk while we think of something else. Instead of paying attention and asking for further clarification, we simply pretend to pay attention.

3 Jumping to conclusions. We think we know what the speaker is going to say, so we "tune out" the message—and often walk away with the wrong understanding.

4 Being prejudiced. Listeners who decide they don't care for the speaker—for any reason—often do not give the speaker a chance. That's why some politicians and controversial figures are "shouted down" when they're prepared to give a talk. Most often, we simply ignore the message.

5 Selective listening. Sometimes, we hear only what we want to hear. Of course, when we do this, we fail to receive the entire message.

6 Apprehension. If we're involved in an argument with a speaker, whom we feel is about to prove us wrong, we might choose not to listen as a defense mechanism.

It has been said that most arguments, conflicts and even wars have resulted from miscommunication. At the very least, faulty communication can cause problems that can hinder your road-building progress.

All of the great leaders of the world have been excellent communicators. They phrased their messages to appeal to the masses and to inspire a following. Mastering good communication skills can help expedite the construction of your road and even gain support for your cause along the way.

PRIORITIZE YOUR LIFE

You've heard it said that if something is worth doing, it's worth doing well. To a point, that's true. But it doesn't mean that everything we do should get equal attention.

Living is a series of priorities. Some things are more important than others. It's our job to determine the things that are most important to us, the things that are least important and those that rank somewhere in-between.

Salespeople apply priorities to their clients. People they feel are most likely to purchase rate an "A" priority. Clients who might buy rate a "B." Those who have indicated a passing interest, but nothing more, rate a "C," and those who have shown little interest at all rate a "D."

When salespeople go to work, they spend most of their time with their "A" clients—the ones most likely to purchase. The "B" clients are not overlooked, because they might become "A" clients with a little effort. "C" clients get attention when they can be conveniently worked into the salesperson's schedule, and "D" clients are paid visits during slow times when salespeople have nothing better to do.

Obviously, salespeople who spend the greatest part of their days with "C" and "D" clients won't be looking out for their best interests.

No matter what we do for a living, we must set priorities like salespeople. Our "A" and "B" activities should be those that will help us build our roads closer to our destinations. Activities that result in little or no growth to our roads should rate "Cs" and "Ds."

BE DECISIVE

Of course, to set priorities, we must make decisions. Sometimes, that can be difficult, especially when we're not sure what the outcome of these decisions might be.

It's easy to agonize over our priorities and other difficult decisions. It's even easier to postpone making a decision, which is a decision to do nothing. And, of course, nothing gets done.

Remember, we will make occasional mistakes in the building of our roads. We're not perfect. But worse than making a mistake and learning from it is making the mistake of doing nothing—and learning nothing at all.

Good leaders are decisive. They weigh all available facts, make decisions and get on with the task of building their roads. If their decisions prove to be wrong, they learn from their mistakes, which will help them build better roads.

If we don't make decisions, our roads go nowhere. If we postpone our decisions long enough, our roads actually might take U-turns. We'll lose progress in our construction toward our destination, and it will take a lot of effort to get them headed back in the right direction.

Be decisive. People without direction are slow to make decisions and are quick to change them. On the other hand, good leaders are quick to make decisions and are slow to change them.

TIME MANAGEMENT

Perhaps the people who are best at self-directed leadership are those who practice good time management.

Let me point out that the practice of time management does not necessarily mean that the 16 or more of your waking hours are devoted to income-producing activities. Good time management simply means using your time doing the things you want to do. If you want to devote all of your time to making money, it's your road. On the other hand, if your idea of life, liberty and happiness involves other activities—even if it's just watching TV and vegetating for three hours on a Sunday afternoon— good time management is simply making sure that you set aside time for those activities. You're responsible for defining your own success, and practicing good time management will help you achieve it, regardless of what you are in the process of accomplishing.

So let me offer you some extremely effective time-management principles that can help you make sure that your time is spent doing the things you want to do. Good time management involves keeping a:

1 Running to-do list. This is the first step to practicing good time management. This list should include anything and everything you want to do. Make a note of activities as they come to mind. If you want to go skiing when winter rolls around, put it down. If you have an activity at work that needs your attention, make a note of it. Keep it where you can see it.

2 Daily to-do list. This is a list of activities for the day. By reviewing your running to-do list and being aware of your daily responsibilities, you can make a daily list of activities that must be handled. And don't forget your priorities. Make sure all "A" priorities get attention over your "B" priorities. Don't worry about your "C" and "D" priorities. Save them for another day, when they become "A" or "B" priorities.

3 Schedule. Once you've determined what is most important for you to do, make a schedule. Assign specific time periods for each event. If possible, build flexible time into your schedule. Should an event take longer than planned, you can then look at your schedule and determine where the "lost" time can be recovered (such as trimming a lunch hour or shaving time from a less demanding activity).

4 Time log. This will help us make better use of our time. When we record how we spend each 15-minute increment of the day, we can determine what we do with our time. Then we can work to improve our use of time by eliminating habits such as procrastination, excessive socializing and too much daydreaming. Of course, no cheating is allowed. If a 10-minute coffee break stretches out to 23 minutes, make a note of it. It's vital to be honest when keeping a time log. Otherwise, it's wasted effort and a poor use of time altogether. Use your time log as a fun activity. Otherwise, it may become tedious. Then use it as a planning guide to get the most out of your day.

The better we use our time, the faster we can build our roads to reach our destinations. Develop good time-management habits to help you realize your self-defined success.

START BUILDING AND KEEP BUILDING

The law of inertia states that an object in motion tends to remain in motion, in the same speed and in the same direction unless it meets with resistance from an outside force. That's one reason that a car gets better mileage during an interstate trip—when a speed is reached and maintained for a long distance—than it does in town, when it's necessary to start and stop repeatedly.

People also are affected by the law of inertia. Once in motion, we tend to remain in motion. But when we stop to rest, it takes more energy to get us going again than we would have used had we remained in motion.

I'm not saying that we can't rest during the day. But we can accomplish more for our energy—or get better mileage, if you prefer—by keeping "brakes" to a minimum.

When building your road, don't be averse to stopping and smelling the roses along the way. That's part of what makes living worthwhile. Just don't take many naps in the rosebeds. It can get to be a habit that can postpone your arrival at your destination.

Master these principles of self-directed leadership, and you'll not only be amazed at how quickly you can reach your destination, but you also might be amazed at the number of people who will want to join you.

And that takes us to the final chapter of the book. Once you've learned to lead yourself, the only thing left to be done is to learn how to lead others. This is a talent you will want to develop when people show interest in joining you in the construction of your road—wherever it might lead.

13

Leadership—Building Roads for Others

> Leadership is the art of getting someone else to do something that you want done because he wants to do it.
> —DWIGHT DAVID EISENHOWER

Once you're well on your way to reaching your destination, there will be others who will be looking to you for guidance. Perhaps they'll be subordinates. Or they might be people who are thinking about following in your footsteps and are looking to you as a role model.

It's a funny thing about self-directed leadership. Once we master it, we automatically gain the admiration and attention of others.

Today's manager must learn to become a leader. People don't want to follow a manager, but they'll rush to follow a leader. When we see someone who knows where he or she is going and it happens to be in the same direction we want to go, we willingly jump right in line.

Let me point out that there is a difference between followers and "tag-alongs." Followers are people who support and share a leader's vision. "Tag-alongs" are people who jump on the bandwagon because they perceive that it's the "in" thing to do. I chose not to jump on the Equal Rights Amendment (ERA) bandwagon during the 1970's. I made the decision not because I didn't support women's rights, which I do. I believed I could make a more powerful statement by making a solid contribution in my role as a Department of Defense employee.

This is not at all to say that women who supported ERA were wrong. The movement was supported by massive numbers of conscientious women whose self-defined success included a vision of seeing the proposal become law of the land. Even though I chose not to get involved, I admire those women for pursuing their self-defined success. These women were true followers in every sense of the word. They supported a vision and were dedicated to bring it to reality.

But the movement also attracted a number of name-dropping "hangers-on"—people who felt prestige in affiliation with pro-ERA forces more than they felt the need for the amendment itself. These were people who knew they "believed" in the ERA but couldn't for the life of them say why. They were building a road to a destination they hadn't even explored because they perceived it to be a popular course of action.

It takes a lot of courage not to jump onto a bandwagon simply because the crowd is doing it. After all, the bandwagon might be headed in a direction we don't want to go. During the mid–1970's, a newly discovered serum was hailed as a vaccine against the dreaded "swine flu" epidemic. Although most drugs are tested by the Food and Drug Administration for years before they are released, this serum was immediately made available to the public. People were lining up for shots, and some employers were strongly urging employees to take them. Even President Gerald Ford was photographed allegedly receiving an injection of the serum.

Suddenly, the program was cancelled in mid-session. Little if any explanation was given. In this case, the people who jumped onto the bandwagon by getting the injections found that they couldn't jump off. The serum was in their systems, and they were going to have to ride the bandwagon until it reached wherever it was going. I'm not aware if there have been any reports of adverse reactions to the injections. I certainly hope none result. But the people who refused to take the shots, I'm sure, can't help but feel a little smug—not to mention re-lieved—with their decisions.

If we want to reach a destination that will make us happy and fulfilled, it's essential for us to define the goal. No one else can take us where we want to go. We have to build our own roads leading to self-defined des-tinations.

Good leaders can show people how to lead themselves, and people who have determined their own destinations can be helped along their way by others who have already built roads in similar directions.

LEADERSHIP HAS ITS BENEFITS

Aside from the intrinsic value of serving as guiding forces in others' lives, there are additional benefits to serving as a capable leader. You might have heard it said before that we can get anything we want by helping other people get what they want. It's true. Successful salespeople subscribe to this principle. They earn enormous incomes by helping clients realize a desire to own what they are selling.

The principle applies in all phases of life. If our only interest in another is in serving as a mentor, we can earn a friendship, respect and trust by showing our protege how to succeed. If our interest in other people extends to a superior-subordinate relationship, we can build our worth to a company—not to mention our income—by showing our subordinates how to succeed.

HELP PEOPLE DEVELOP BY "KNIGHTING" THEM

Remember the lesson we learned from the *Wizard of Oz*. People have all the potential they need to succeed in their chosen endeavors. They don't need to be "knighted" by a higher source.

But that doesn't change the fact that people might feel that they need to be knighted. Sure, people have great potential. But, sometimes, poor self-esteem effectively blocks their ability to turn their potential into productivity. If we, as leaders, treat the people who would follow us as though they are royal, wonderful and worthwhile, they'll act that way—just like the scarecrow, tin man and cowardly lion responded to the honors the wizard bestowed upon them.

The best way we can "knight" those who would follow us is by understanding the four stages of the learning process and by directing them through each phase of development. These stages apply whenever we undertake any new endeavor.

1 Unconscious incompetent. Even when we know we don't know anything about a new task, we somehow believe we'll learn fast. It seems to be human nature to have a good attitude about something we're about to learn even before we begin. We're incompetent at this stage, but we don't realize it.

2 Conscious incompetent. At this point, we've gotten our feet wet, and we realize the water is not very comfortable. Once we begin to learn how to do something, we realize that it's not as easy as it looks. At this point, it's easy to give up, because we're incompetent, and we know it.

3 Conscious competent. If we stick with a task, we'll eventually learn how to perform well. But good performance will require full concentration. Because we lack sufficient experience, the process hasn't been committed to our subconscious minds. So competent performance is still a conscious effort.

4 Unconscious competent. Once we've gained sufficient experience at doing something right, we can do it practically with our eyes closed. We're competent even when we're thinking about something else.

By understanding these four stages of educational development, you can effectively lead people to success in any given endeavor. It all depends on how you relate to them while they're in each phase, which leads us to . . .

THE FOUR EFFECTIVE LEADERSHIP STYLES

Leaders don't treat all followers the same, because all followers don't have the same levels of experience. We can't treat unconscious incompetents the way we treat unconscious competents, or they would never develop into capable people.

Let's take a look at four styles that effective leaders use when relating to subordinates in varying stages of development.

1 Tell style. This is the most effective leadership style to use when dealing with unconscious incompetents. They don't know anything about the task, so they must be told how to perform. But they also aren't fully aware of how much they don't know, so they usually are eager to begin work. This means that they need little if any encouragement to get started. So we can best describe the tell style of management as a combination of high directive and low supportive behaviors.

2 Sell style. Interaction between the leader and subordinate peaks at this stage. The subordinate becomes aware of his or her incompetence. Not only must the leader continue to provide detailed instruction, but the subordinate in this phase of development most often needs moral support. The effective leader ''sells'' the conscious incompetent on his or her ability to perform well. The sell style of management involves a mixture of high directive and high supportive behaviors.

3 Join style. This style of management is directed toward the conscious competent. The leader can cut back, or eliminate altogether, directive behavior, since the subordinate knows how to perform. But it's necessary to maintain high supportive behavior, because the subordinate still is less than comfortable with his or her performance. With this style, the leader "joins" the subordinate by offering moral support and encouragement.

4 Delegate style. When the subordinate is fully prepared to handle a task competently, the leader can simply delegate. This involves assigning a job and allowing the subordinate to decide how best to perform it. No directive behavior is necessary, and neither is supportive behavior. The subordinate is an unconscious competent, and he or she needs no further assistance.

While the leader takes the subordinate through the four stages of development, it is wise to recognize that people have different needs when it comes to decision-making, quality, stability, change and social interaction. One major error I've seen by managers and supervisors is the cloning of themselves in organizations. Strength lies in building a team which complements the talents of each team member and the manager.

By responding sensitively and appropriately to the needs of those who would follow us, we can build strong followers with minimal effort. That means that we can devote more attention to building our own personal roads. Everybody involved prospers.

MODIFY BEHAVIOR THROUGH
APPROPRIATE CONSEQUENCES

Parents sometimes find it easy to lecture, scold and sometimes scream at their children to encourage them to behave properly. Seldom, if ever, does it produce positive results.

There's a better way to guide children and subordinates, too. It's called behavior modification.

Psychiatrists and psychologists operate on the principle that when someone isn't behaving properly, it's important to find out why. Once the antecedent, or the impetus for a particular behavior, is discovered and the individual is informed, the behavior can be more easily modified.

Of course, discovering the antecedent for behavior can involve a long, tedious and sometimes expensive process. Behavior modification offers a better and faster solution. With this strategy, the antecedent is not important. Effective leaders cannot afford to be overly concerned with why a person chooses to behave improperly; they are only concerned with modifying the behavior.

In most cases, this can be done by establishing appropriate consequences for various behaviors. For example, negative behavior that meets with neutral consequences will, in all likelihood, be repeated. If children learn they can violate curfew without fear of reprisal, they'll continue to violate it. Likewise, if followers discover they can break certain rules without adverse consequences, they'll continue to break rules.

When negative behavior is met with negative consequences, there's a good chance the negative behavior won't be repeated.

Of course, children and followers will behave positively, too. And it's a vital that they meet with the appropriate consequences. Unlike negative behavior, positive conduct that meets with neutral consequences likely will not be repeated. On the other hand, positive behavior that is rewarded with positive consequences might become a habit.

Effective leaders keep track of their followers' behaviors and provide appropriate consequences. It's vital for building strong, effective followers.

BUILD A BETTER WORLD BY BUILDING OTHERS

Aside from helping others improve, and improving ourselves in the process, we help to build a better world through effective leadership. A neighborhood is no better than its residents, and that holds true for the community, the city, the state, the country and even the world.

Regardless of your field of endeavor or what role you play as a leader, here are some tips you can use to help people develop.

1 Understand the law of self-fulfilling prophecy. In the first chapter, we discussed the significance self-esteem plays in an individual's development. We also discussed in Chapter Nine how mentors can influence their proteges with the verbal feedback they give them. Putting the two together, we have the law of self-fulfilling prophecy. When someone we respect gives us positive feedback, our self-esteem improves, and we act positively. But when feedback is negative, our self-esteem suffers, and we respond by acting negatively. In short, we will live up or down to the expectations of the people whose opinions we respect. Bear this in mind in your relationships with your followers.

2 Trust your followers. This principle relates to the law of self-fulfilling prophecy. If we trust our followers, they'll act in a trustworthy manner. If we don't trust them, they will prove that we were right.

3 Accept relationships and situations in terms of present and future—not the past. Don't let an unpleasant incident or situation in the past cloud your current and future relationship with a follower. Even if someone has acted improperly in the past, if he or she hasn't committed an impardonable sin worthy of dismissal or disassociation, then he or she is worth another chance, and should be treated as a first-class citizen. Remember, no value judging allowed. The antecedent for the behavior isn't important. If the behavior can be forgiven, the slate should be wiped clean. If the behavior can't be forgiven, then the relationship should be terminated.

4 Live what you talk. Nothing will destroy respect for a leader any faster than hypocrisy. People who don't abide by the principles they espouse for others can't even lead themselves. Why should other people follow them. If you would be a leader, it's vital that you "live your talk." Your effectiveness as a leader depends on it.

By helping others develop into more productive, capable people, we make our contribution to the Supreme Commissioner of Highways, who created the world and all of its residents and who watches over each of us as we build our roads.

The Commissioner cares about your road and the destination you choose. Sometimes, even leaders need leaders. If ever in doubt about your direction, don't be averse to asking for guidance. The Commissioner will show you the way.

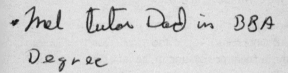

Epilogue

People who build their own roads enjoy incredible success in life. They do more than earn a living. They take an appealing vision and turn it into reality. Accomplishing success renews them so much more than a mere paycheck. Success begets more success. Once a vision becomes reality, the only thing left to do is to create a new vision and turn it into reality. Such is the course of a fulfilling life road.

While building your road, I would like you to consider certain "features" to include which will make your effort enjoyable and rewarding.

1 Entry and Exit Ramps. These are necessary to get you on and off the road as you desire. Sometimes, you will want to get off the career road and work on the vacation road or family road. Remember, the best success involves success at building all of your roads.

2 A Slow Lane. Circumstances or other obligations can periodically prevent us from making a great deal of progress on our roads. Build flexible time into your schedules to allow for occasional life in the slow lane.

3 A Fast Lane. Life in this lane can be exciting when conditions are clear and you are bursting with energy. Just be sure you don't travel too fast to accomplish your goals and miss the joy of progress.

4 A Carpool Lane. This is for times when you need the assistance of others, and when they need you. Remember, we need other people to succeed.

5 An Emergency Lane. Again, build flexible time into your plans. Life has a way of throwing us "engine troubles" and "flat tires" when we least expect them. Try to foresee emergencies, and be prepared to handle them.

6 A Rest Area. Don't forget to take short "time outs" for rest stops and pleasant distractions. This stop also is good for refueling the body and mind.

7 A Weigh Station. Visit this stop whenever it's necessary to measure the burden of your decisions and their impact on yourself and others.

8 A Dump Truck. No good road builder should be without a suitable vehicle to dispose of unnecessary debris. Use your truck to dump your worries and nonproductive second thoughts.

Here are four general rules to follow in building your road.

1 Decorate your road. Plant some trees, grass and flowers along the way. Lend a helping hand to someone in need. Do a favor for someone. Then do another one.

Let your road indicate that life is wonderful, and that people are beautiful.

2 Visit other people's roads. Invite other people to visit yours. When two roads intersect, both builders can benefit. There is no need to compare your road with someone else's. Enjoy your road, and other people's roads, too.

3 Avoid reckless "drivers." These are people you meet whose actions and behavior would jeopardize your chances of reaching your destination.

4 Drive carefully. When your road is dark, don't overdrive your headlights. When conditions are stormy, slow down. Be aware of what lies ahead of you, so you can avoid potholes and road blocks that might cause you unnecessary delay.

No matter what destination you choose, be willing to build your own road leading to it. This may place you in a minority. However, people who are willing to bring to reality their visions of success will always be the most capable, competent and effective. That's why there will always be a great demand for road builders.

Good luck with your road, and happy traveling. And if this book plays a part in helping you reach your destination, please send me a postcard.

What do I really want
out of life.

What does success actually
mean to me.

What do I can want to d
when I retire.

when do I want to retire

what do I need in place
when I retire

For Further
Information

For information on Lois' availability to speak at your next meeting, or for questions regarding this book and other Lois Wolfe-Morgan products, write Wolfe Associates, P.O. Box 404, Plymouth, Michigan 48170 or call (313) 420–2906.

BE A WINNER!
with these books by
DR. DENIS WAITLEY

___**THE DOUBLE WIN** 0-425-08530-9/$4.50
For anyone who has the desire to excel, here's
how to get to the top without putting others down.

___**THE WINNER'S EDGE** 0-425-10000-6/$4.50
How to develop your success potential, by the
man who has made a career of helping others get
ahead.

___**THE PSYCHOLOGY OF WINNING**
0-425-09999-7/$4.50
Learn the ten vital secrets of success—from self-
awareness, to self-projection!

THE #1 NATIONAL BESTSELLERS—
BE SURE YOU'VE READ THEM BOTH!

The One Minute Manager
and its essential follow-up
Putting The One Minute Manager To Work

__THE ONE MINUTE MANAGER
   Kenneth Blanchard, Ph.D. and Spencer Johnson, M.D.
   0-425-09847-8/$8.50
Whether you manage a multinational corporation or a suburban
household, THE ONE MINUTE MANAGER is guaranteed to
change your life. Using three easy-to-follow techniques, it shows you
how to increase your productivity, save time, and get the most from
your job, your family, and yourself...(Large Format)

__PUTTING THE ONE MINUTE MANAGER TO WORK
   Kenneth Blanchard, Ph.D. and Robert Lorber, Ph.D.
   0-425-10425-7/$8.95
This essential follow-up applies the secret of ONE MINUTE GOAL
SETTING, ONE MINUTE PRAISINGS and ONE MINUTE
REPRIMANDS to REAL-LIFE SITUATIONS...so that you can put
them to work in your life immediately! (Large Format)

237